"Sorry," Jensen breathed, the warmth of her breath skating across his cheek. "I got a bit dizzy. I haven't slept much the past few days."

Cristiano's hand splayed across her bottom, holding her securely. And suddenly, those erotic images he'd envisioned waking up to replayed themselves in his head in vivid Technicolor detail. Except this time, he knew what she felt like, and he wasn't certain it was an image he could get out of his head.

Moving his hand up to a more respectable position at her waist, he set her away from him. That inconvenient chemistry flared between them, dark eyes fixed on blue, smoking up the air between them for a long, infinitesimal second, before she slicked her tongue over her lips in a nervous movement and stepped back, his arm dropping away from her waist.

"Thank you," she murmured in a husky voice. "That could have been a nasty fall."

He doused the heat snaking through his body with a superhuman effort, because *this* was not happening between them. He was here to enforce the rules. Nothing more.

Jennifer Hayward has been a fan of romance since filching her sister's novels to escape her teenage angst. Her career in journalism and PR, including years of working alongside powerful, charismatic CEOs and traveling the world, has provided perfect fodder for the fast-paced, sexy stories she likes to write—always with a touch of humor. A native of Canada's East Coast, Jennifer lives in picturesque Nova Scotia with her Viking husband and teenage Viking-in-training.

Books by Jennifer Hayward

Harlequin Presents

A Debt Paid in the Marriage Bed
Salazar's One-Night Heir

The Billionaire's Legacy

A Deal for the Di Sione Ring

The Powerful Di Fiore Tycoons

Christmas at the Tycoon's Command
His Million-Dollar Marriage Proposal
Married for His One-Night Heir

Visit the Author Profile page
at Harlequin.com for more titles.

Jennifer Hayward

HOW THE ITALIAN CLAIMED HER

HARLEQUIN
PRESENTS

Recycling programs
for this product may
not exist in your area.

ISBN-13: 978-1-335-59196-8

How the Italian Claimed Her

Copyright © 2023 by Jennifer Drogell

For questions and comments about the quality of this book,
please contact us at CustomerService@Harlequin.com.

Harlequin Enterprises ULC
22 Adelaide St. West, 41st Floor
Toronto, Ontario M5H 4E3, Canada
www.Harlequin.com

Printed in U.S.A.

HOW THE ITALIAN
CLAIMED HER

This one is for you, Dottie Auletto. No one could have been a bigger Harlequin Presents fan or loved books more than you did. I'm heartbroken that you're gone. I miss you so much. But your love of romance and your amazing spirit will always be with me as I write. xx

CHAPTER ONE

CRISTIANO VITALE HAD just consumed a fortifying, and more importantly eye-opening, sip of strong, dark espresso when his chief marketing officer appeared in his office, looking far more frazzled than the holder of such a position should be, just weeks out from the launch of the most important collection in Francesco Vitale's storied history.

Founded over a half century ago by his late grandfather, Francesco Vitale, the legendary Italian fashion house he commanded was on the verge of a massive rebirth, a do-or-die moment for the company he'd spent a decade rebuilding. What had necessitated a 4:00 a.m. start to the morning that he was presently attempting to wake up from. Putting out another fire before he'd even gotten to his emails wasn't how he particularly wanted to start the day. He was sure, however, from the frustration written across Antonio Braga's inordinately stressed face that he had no choice in the matter.

He sat back in his chair, hands wrapped around his coffee cup, and motioned his CMO into the chair opposite him. "You have five minutes before I'm due in a meeting with the lawyers. Make it quick."

Antonio ignored the chair he offered and paced to the window, where he stood, staring out at a magnificent view of Milan, every muscle in his perfectly groomed body tense, his shoulders practically up at his ears. "I need you to do me a favor."

Cristiano hiked a brow. An interesting way to start the conversation, given the power differential between the two, and given that his CMO knew the weight he was presently carrying. But as he'd never seen Antonio this out of sorts before, he elected to play along. "Which is?"

Antonio turned and leaned a hip against the windowsill, his handsome face haggard and lined with the strain he'd been carrying for months. "You are in London tonight?"

"Si." An in-and-out-in-a-night business trip he would prefer not to do, but one that was key. "Why?" he queried. "You need to tag along?"

"No." Antonio raked a hand through his short dark hair, looking as if that idea horrified him. "I have an ad campaign to finish and a television commercial to shoot, and no time to do either." A silence followed as he set his gaze on Cristiano. "It's Jensen Davis."

The hairs on the back of Cristiano's neck rose. The wild-child face of his brand, American supermodel Jensen Davis, had been causing havoc for him for weeks, racking up headlines faster than the millions he paid her. Scandalous, *salacious* headlines with the power to sully the FV legacy at a time when it could least afford it.

A dark current of frustration sizzled up his spine. "What has she done now?" he growled.

Antonio deposited the entertainment section of one of London's daily newspapers on his desk. Cristiano set his coffee cup down and pulled the newspaper toward him. The front page of the section featured a photo of the twenty-six-year-old Jensen stumbling out of a club, dressed in a jaw-dropping red dress, in what looked like the early hours of the morning.

Her luxurious chestnut-colored hair fell in a silken curtain over her shoulder; her stunning ebony eyes emphasized with dark, smoky makeup that made them look undeniably haunting, her sensational body encased in a body-hugging silk, she was the most unforgettably beautiful woman he'd ever set eyes on. The perfect canvas for the FV brand.

He scanned the text beneath the photograph, his trepidation mounting.

Catwalk Catfight!
Jensen Davis, the hottest model on the catwalk, continued her headline-grabbing behavior of late, engaging in a very public catfight with Princess Juliana Margues last night at Zoro. Rumored to be a disagreement over Davis's nude romp in an Italian fountain with Prince Alexandre of Santeval, the princess's on-again, off-again beau.
After the spirited exchange, which featured a shouting match and a drink Margues purportedly threw at Davis, the American supermodel made a quick exit with her entourage.
One can only wonder how far this will go before the palace steps in. Bets are it won't be too long.
Meanwhile, Davis is set to headline the Designer Extravaganza in support of the London Hospital Foundation this evening, the most coveted ticket in town.

Cristiano's blood heated in his veins. The fountain incident in Rome had been bad enough, given his family's close personal ties to the pope, and the resulting scandal that had followed. Now Davis was instigating a full royal PR response? There was a line, he breathed. A line to these antics of hers she couldn't cross, and she'd done it twice in the past few weeks. *Infuriating*, when he'd been reassured she'd left her irresponsible behavior behind. Promised she was a professional now.

He drew in a deep breath. Tempered the wave of dark heat scorching through him. "I told you to take care of this, Antonio. It is too much. *Troppo.*"

"I've tried," his CMO defended hotly, a swath of color climbing his aristocratic cheekbones, "but she is a moving target. And her agent has been no help."

"Because she is out of control," Cristiano thundered, jabbing a long finger at the photograph. "Racking up thirty-thousand-euro bar tabs in Monaco on wild nights of partying... *Debasing* sacred fountains in Rome... Blowing off her FV responsibilities. Pascal is ready to lose his marbles," he said, referring to his brand-new star designer, set to take his grandfather's place as the creative head of the company. "He can't finish the collection without her. She is a *phantom*," he breathed, waving a hand in the air, "appearing only when she likes."

His CMO scrubbed a palm over his brow.

"She's usually a complete professional when it comes to her work. I have no idea what's going on with her. How to deal with this."

Cristiano pushed the newspaper away, frustration singeing his fingertips. He'd been content to look the other way at some of Davis's attention-grabbing stunts, because they only tended to increase her popularity, and thus that of the FV brand. But these latest exploits? They had the potential to do real damage to both her own brand and Francesco Vitale's if they continued. Not to mention the shirking of her FV responsibilities, something he would never tolerate.

"Need I remind you," he bit out, his gaze resting on his marketing chief, "that we have bet the bank on her, Antonio? That she is the centerpiece of *everything* we have created? That I went against Francesco's express wishes on this because of *your* recommendation, a decision that likely has him turning in his grave?"

"Which I stand firm on," his CMO replied staunchly. "Jensen Davis is the most important influencer on the face of the planet when it comes to the millennials we need to capture if this company is to survive. Young women aspire to *be* her, Cristiano. She is making our clothes aspirational again. Our brand relevancy scores have doubled since she came aboard."

"Which will plummet into the nether if she continues like this."

"I won't let that happen," Antonio assured him, his elegantly shaved square jaw flexing. "Yes, it's been a rough few weeks. But she will deliver. She always does."

Cristiano exhaled a deep breath. He had hired Davis, whom his grandfather had not approved of, the "it" girl of her generation, the most recognizable face in America from her days as a fashion-obsessed teenager on her Hollywood family's reality show, to make the Francesco Vitale brand relevant again. But it wasn't a decision he'd made lightly.

He had balked at the idea of hiring Davis when his marketing team first put her name forward, sure that with her wild-child history she'd be more trouble than she was worth. But he hadn't been able to deny the influence she'd held over the fashion world. Nor the power she wielded over the prevailing pop culture. He'd agreed to go see a shoot she was doing, sure he would talk himself out of it by the time he'd left the room. Instead, he'd found himself as beguiled as everyone else in attendance by her beauty. Fascinated by the untamed free spirit she'd been, a life she could breathe into the stagnating Francesco Vitale brand, which badly needed a jolt of fresh air. By the magic she'd created in front of the camera.

His gut had told him she was *it*—a battle he'd waged with his grandfather, who'd favored a traditional Italian model versus the wild card Jensen had represented, until his grandfather had reluctantly acquiesced. A decision he was now having to second-guess, given Davis's erratic behavior. Exasperating, because he didn't have *time* to be questioning any part of his ambitious plan. When he'd been promised Davis's behavior would not be an issue.

He pinned a look on Antonio, framed in the sunshine of a magnificent Milanese morning rapidly losing its rosy glow. "What is your plan? I assume you have one."

"*Si.*" Antonio reached up to tug at his tie and loosen it, an uncharacteristically nervous gesture for his ultra-confident, brilliant marketing guru. "I thought you might attend the Designer Extravaganza tonight. Talk to Jensen. Impart on her the *importance* of the next few weeks for the company. Coming from you, I thought it would have more impact. Unless," he added hesitantly, casting a wary glance at Cristiano's smoldering expression, "you would like me to come with you and do it myself."

Cristiano rubbed a palm over the stubble on his jaw, a task he hadn't had five minutes to see to this morning. He did not have the *capacity* for this. He had three major crises raging on two different continents and an outdated supply chain making his life hell. A major investment deal he needed to land in order to make it all happen, which wasn't at all a sure thing at the moment, not to mention a dozen other minor fires he had waiting to put out. He didn't have time to *breathe*. But with everything resting on Pascal Ferrari's debut collection for FV, the first by his grandfather's successor, a campaign in which Davis sat squarely at the center of, he had no choice but to step in.

If neither his CMO nor Davis's agent could control his star asset, he would. Because with Jensen Davis at the heart of his plans to reinvent Francesco Vitale, failure was not an option.

He eyed Antonio across the desk, a steel-edged sense of purpose lancing through him. "Focus on the campaign. I will deal with Davis."

Jensen Davis absorbed the frantic backstage atmosphere at the historic, glamorous Guildhall in London with a brain so bleary with fatigue, it felt like it was stuffed with cotton wool. Usually, in these last few moments before a show, the electric anticipation of those adrenaline-packed few moments on stage provided her with the charge she needed for the patented high-energy performance she was known for, what had propelled her to the status of the world's top model. Tonight, however, she was operating on only four hours' sleep, half of what she required to feel vaguely human, so drained by the prior month's relentless schedule she was shocked she even knew what city she was in.

Registering her current location might have been easier on this particular occasion than others, if only for the fact that she'd had to fight her way through a crowd of paparazzi as she'd left her hotel, each of them demanding to know about last night's altercation with Princess Juliana, a scene she would prefer to forget.

Jensen, what do you have to say about Princess Juliana's claim you've stolen her fiancé?

What does it feel like to be a relationship-wrecker?

Are you having an affair with Prince Alex?

What does the palace think of all of this?

Baseball cap jammed on her head, sunglasses shading her eyes from the glare of the flash-bulbs, she'd ignored them all and slid into the back seat of the waiting car. But she wasn't fool-ish enough to think it would end there. There would be months of tabloid headlines. Endless speculation. Ridiculous drama manufactured by a royal-obsessed press that couldn't seem to get enough of the story.

All because she'd given in to her mother's desperate plea for one last favor before her show, *Hollywood Divas,* went on hiatus. Her mother, a fading silver screen legend, divided her time between her infamous on-and off-screen exploits, perfect fodder for the wildly popular reality show she starred in each week along with a supporting cast of former A-list stars. Only now, since Jensen and her sisters had left the show, refusing to participate in the stunts her mother pulled as they each pursued their own careers and a life outside of television, the ratings for the decade-long-running show had plummeted, with the producers threatening to cancel the series unless a season finale stunt could provide a major boost to the numbers.

Jensen, determined to maintain her distance from the life she'd left behind, had flatly refused to even consider the whole fountain stunt, until her mother had broken down in tears, sobbing that she'd have nothing left if the show was gone, too. That she'd be flat broke. Which Jensen knew was true, since she'd been bankrolling her mother for the past eighteen months, her mother promising to *do better* each time, which never seemed to happen. Nor could she ask for help from her sisters, Ava and Scarlett, who had founded a fledgling design business and boutique in Manhattan, with no extra money to spare. Which meant all of this fell on her.

Which she might have been able to handle if she wasn't also dealing with the aftereffects of her mother's big end-of-season stunt. The *fountain episode,* which continued to haunt Jensen, even in her sleep.

What had started out as an innocent stunt involving a historic fountain in Rome and a midnight skinny-dipping episode with her good friend, Alex, had seemed harmless enough. Until he'd used it as a tactic to get his ex-fiancée back. Little had she known that Alex planned to leave her hanging in the wind amid rumors of an affair, refusing to correct the salacious headlines that had raged, in the hopes that Juliana would come running back to him. Which, judging from the princess's behavior the night before, she was about to do.

"I did you a favor," Alex had protested when she'd called to ask him to step in. To quell the rumors. "I saved the show." Which technically was true, with the ratings for the season finale the highest of any network television show this season, guaranteeing her mother yet another year on the air. But what about *her*? Her reputation? That professionalism she'd worked so hard to cultivate? She had not signed on for this. A tabloid firestorm that was burning out of control.

Jacob, her hairstylist, finished the last big curl of her Hollywood-inspired style and doused her with a cloud of hair spray. She closed her eyes in the briefest of respites. Really, she should have known better. The media always twisted the facts to fit whatever they were looking for; she a favorite target for their keyboards. Not to mention the fact that giving in to her mother was always an exercise in futility. It always created more problems than it solved.

At the end of the day, this was *her* fault.

"But really," Lucy Parker, a British model with a wicked wit, tossed at her as they were given the ten-minute warning by the showrunner. "What *is* going on between you and Alexandre? You can tell me. I won't say a thing. You can't possibly just be friends."

"We are," Jensen responded wearily, for what seemed like the hundredth time. "Why is that so hard to believe?"

"Because he's gorgeous… The heir to a fortune. And you were naked in that fountain together."

"We weren't naked. I had lingerie on." Something the press *hadn't* seen fit to print. "And it was just a lark." One she wished badly she could take back now.

"Who cares about Prince Alexandre?" Millie, one of the French models interrupted, arriving at their side in a swish of gossamer fabric. "Cristiano Vitale is here. *Mon Dieu*," she breathed, "he is the hottest man I have ever laid eyes on. Beautiful, but not so beautiful he's perfect. Beautiful in the *manly* sense. I met him once and I couldn't even look at him straight. He is so amazing. He's completely intimidating."

Jensen's stomach dropped to the floor. *Cristiano Vitale was here? Why?* FV didn't have a presence here tonight. Nor was it customary for the CEO of the company to attend these types of things. Her mind flew back to the salacious headlines of the past few weeks. The rather panicked text she'd received from her agent on the way over here tonight, a text she hadn't answered because she'd been running late.

CALL ME, was all it had said.

"You would have the scoop." Millie fixed an avaricious gaze on Jensen. "Is he here with anyone? What's his status?"

"I'm not sure." She hadn't seen Cristiano Vitale since her very first shoot for the company, at which he'd lorded over the proceedings like the king of England. She'd gotten the distinct impression he'd been there to make sure he hadn't blown his millions on a piece of reality show trash. She'd never gotten such an infuriatingly arrogant impression in her life.

"He's supposed to marry the beautiful socialite Alessandra Grasso," a Spanish model pointed out. "I wouldn't pin your hopes on that one."

"They are on-again, off-again," Millie tossed back. "And right now, they are *off*. He is fair game."

"I would give it a go," Lucy said, fanning herself with a handheld mirror. "I bet it would be worth every minute of the crash and burn."

Jensen was fairly sure it wouldn't be. Not with that overabundant arrogance reigning supreme. She ran damp palms down the skirt of her sleek silver dress, a movement that got her a frown from the showrunner. There were a million reasons Cristiano Vitale could be here, she reasoned. He could be in town on business. He might know someone in attendance. Except, she conceded, this appearance *was* out of the ordinary for him, because rumor had it, he was too busy making the sweeping behind-the-scenes changes at FV she'd quietly applauded if the brand she'd loved ever since she was a teenager were to survive.

The show manager gave them the two-minute warning. Jensen pulled in a steadying breath, attempting to mentally psyche herself up when her legs felt like lead. *Twenty minutes* and this would all be over. All she had to do was put one foot in front of the other until she'd finished her three wardrobe changes and the show was done. She'd give the after-party a ghostly quick visit, get out of here early and get some much-needed sleep before her flight to Paris.

She took her place at the entrance to the stage, the first in line to kick off the night. Absorbed the magnificent, soaring architecture of the gorgeous Gothic hall with its sweeping arches, atmospheric stained-glass windows and five-inch-thick stone walls, lit in purple and silver tonight. The blinding light and the intimate narrow runway, which made putting a foot out of place an inherently disastrous mistake. The packed, buzzing crowd.

"Do some reconnaissance," Lucy whispered in her ear. "Find out where he is."

She would prefer not to. In fact, practically swaying on her feet with exhaustion, she was just hoping to keep her feet on the runway, rather than end up in the crowd.

The music slowly increased in volume, and the lights went down. Adrenaline moved through her veins, transporting her to that magical place where it was just her and the runway ahead. Nothing else. And then, her cue came.

She stepped into the spotlight at the top of the runway. Waited for the crowd to register her appearance with a dramatic pause. Then, as the music reached its peak, she started down the stone walkway with her patented confident prowl, hips sashaying as her long stride ate up the distance, a feminine flourish to her walk her agent liked to call her secret power.

When she reached the end of the runway, she stopped to pose, focusing on showing off the gorgeous dress from every angle, every shimmer of the fabric revealing yet another carefully executed detail. Planted in the space for an extended moment as flashbulbs went off in a blinding cascade, she finally saw *him*.

Seated in the front row alongside the executive director of the show, she felt the full force of Cristiano Vitale's electric-blue gaze as it hit her like a sledgehammer. He moved it over her from tip to toe, taking in the exquisitely designed dress with an utterly unreadable look. But it was his eyes that revealed the barely banked emotion fueling him. He was *furious*. *Incensed*. She could feel it radiating from him like an invisible force. And suddenly, she knew it was no coincidence he was here. Not even a chance.

Her stomach plunged, a flurry of goose bumps unearthing themselves over the surface of her skin. She was in deep trouble. And all she could do was face the music. Literally.

Blowing a kiss to the crowd, she made her way back up the runway for her wardrobe change. Managed to somehow make it through the rest of the show under the force of that furious, cerulean-blue gaze that watched her unblinkingly from the front row. When someone passed her a message after the show that Cristiano Vitale wanted to see her, she wasn't surprised, although that didn't make her any less nervous. She felt a bit sick, actually.

She considered slipping out the back door and not dealing with it at all. But that would redefine the term *career-limiting move*. Could perhaps be a *career*-ending *move*.

Best to get it over with. She left her makeup on, because she felt less vulnerable with it, changed into the gauzy metallic olive-green dress the designer she was wearing tonight had chosen for her, and left her hair loose, falling down her back in a silken cloud. Surveying herself in the mirror, she cursed her unusual pallor before deciding it was the best she was going to do with Cristiano Vitale waiting. At least he couldn't see inside to the knots that were tying her stomach into a ball.

Picking up her clutch, she descended the stairs to the magnificent old crypts located directly beneath the Great Hall, where the after-party was being held.

Usually, this would be the time where she could relax and kick off the stress of the high-intensity evening, but tonight she couldn't seem to do it, her eyes scanning the crowd for a glimpse of Cristiano Vitale.

It didn't take long. If her gaze hadn't been drawn to him, she might simply have followed every other set of female eyes in the room to the man standing leaning against one of the thick pillars that swept up into a series of graceful arches that adorned the room. Dressed in a dark gray three-piece suit that bucked the trend of black in the room, the dove-white shirt he wore gleamed starkly against his swarthy skin, his silver-gray tie the epitome of elegant European style.

Which didn't end with the suit. It was there in the perfectly cut, raven-dark hair slicked back from the hard lines of his face. In the handmade gold cuff links at his wrists. The relaxed, indolent posture that screamed power from its very restraint. Hands thrust into his pockets, the fine material of his suit pulled taut across powerful muscle, he was the most virile, arresting man she'd ever encountered. Smoking hot in a way few women could resist.

Okay, she admitted shakily, so Millie had

been right. He was outrageously good-looking. The only explanation for the mind block she'd been suffering was that she'd blanked it all out at the shoot, because it had been the only way she could maintain her concentration in the face of his extremely distracting presence.

She forced herself to move toward him on legs that suddenly didn't seem to want to work, stopping when she was a mere few inches from him. "Cristiano," she greeted him.

"Jensen," he acknowledged with a dip of his head, the light rasp of his accent working its way under the layers of her skin. He bent his head to brush his mouth against her cheek in a typically Italian caress. Which didn't feel in any way typical to her. It felt nerve jarring and unsettling, in a way she'd never experienced before. She sucked in a breath as he did the same with her other cheek and stepped back. His sapphire gaze fixed on hers, penetrating and unyielding.

He moved it over her from head to foot, taking in the sexy semitransparent dress that revealed a daring amount of bare flesh. Her skin felt singed as he cataloged the deep vee of the provocative neckline and the clever cutouts designed to show off her curves, an involuntary sizzle rippling through her as he returned his gaze to her face, a dark glitter in his eyes. For a split second, she could almost imagine the fury she'd absorbed from him onstage was tinged with another emotion entirely—a pure, unadulterated chemistry that zigzagged between them, so potent it shook her to her toes as it reverberated through her.

Which she must have imagined, she thought shakily, as his long dark lashes swept down to veil his blue gaze, because she was sure anger was his predominant emotion. Which made her wish desperately the designer had chosen something a little more sedate for the evening. Less vamp and more...*sophisticated,* so she didn't feel so exposed. But it was too late for that now.

She straightened her shoulders and tipped her head back to look up at him, refusing to be intimidated. "I—I had no idea you would be here," she stammered, annoyed at herself for the nervous tip of her hand. "That anyone from FV would be here."

"I was in town on business for the day. Richard Worthington is a friend of mine." He took a sip of his drink, savoring the spirit before he leaned back against the wall, his eyes on her. "I also thought that, given the string of headlines you've managed to generate over the past few weeks, it might be a good idea if we chatted."

The ball of nerves in her stomach knotted itself tighter. There it was. The displeasure she'd known was coming. He wasn't wasting time getting to the point, but then again, he didn't strike her as the type of man who would. He was all business, all the time, from what she'd heard. And then, there was that air of combustive energy that seemed to surround him like a glove.

She swallowed past the sudden constriction in her throat. "The media like to blow things up into something they're not. I, unfortunately, seem to be one of their favorite targets."

"Because you make yourself one. You've built a career out of it."

"Well…yes." She sank her teeth into her lip, caught off guard by the scythe-sharp assessment. "That might be true of the past, but not so much of the present."

He arched a dark brow at her. "So you and your entourage didn't rack up a thirty-thousand-euro bar tab in Monaco on a wild night of partying in which hotel rooms were trashed? That was someone else and not you *nude* in the middle of the Trevi Fountain at midnight… A body double, perhaps? And clearly, the drink-throwing incident with the princess was simply a fabric of the press's imagination?"

Hot color doused her cheeks. The bar tab had been her mother's, but that wasn't something she could share, because her mother's drinking and gambling problem was a deep, dark Davis family secret she and her sisters had concealed for over a decade. Nor could she reveal that the fountain stunt had been a product of her mother's desperation, because the fact remained she'd done it. She had no excuse for her behavior. Nor could she deny the drink the princess had thrown at her, though it was hardly the catfight the press had reported it as. It had been more along the lines of Juliana hysterically shouting at her that she'd ruined her life and losing her entire rationality, before she'd thrown the cocktail at her. Which wasn't an impressive explanation either without the accompanying backstory.

Which left an apology her only viable option. "It was an error in judgment," she said quietly. "The past few weeks. You can expect nothing but professionalism from me from now on."

Once the firestorm faded.

Cristiano Vitale gave her a long look. "I think we've gotten to the point where I'm not willing to take your word for it, Ms. Davis. In case you weren't aware of it, I am in the middle of a massive transformation of the FV brand. A transformation which relies on the sanctity and reputation of FV's legacy—a legacy you are currently dragging through the mud."

Jensen blanched. "I wouldn't put it quite like

that. Some would say any publicity is good publicity."

"Not in this case," he slung back, voice razor-sharp. "I was willing to overlook some of your usual antics, because I get that the buzz builds your influencer status and by default my own brand. But there is a line, Ms. Davis. Representatives of the FV brand *do not* drink themselves under the table. They do not indulge in excessively public affairs with royalty, nor do they *debase* national monuments in the country in which Francesco Vitale was founded."

Now he was the one embellishing the narrative. No one had drunk themselves under the table in Monaco, though she was fairly sure her mother had been a mere drink or two away from it. Why she'd felt compelled to drop everything and swoop in and clean up. Nor was she having an affair with Alexandre. In fact, right now she'd rather strangle him. But she was fairly certain, taking in Cristiano Vitale's glittering blue gaze, that providing explanations or arguing the point was likely to have little effect.

"Like I said," she said quietly, "it won't happen again."

"And then," he forged on, as if she hadn't spoken at all, "there are the FV responsibilities you have blown off over the past few weeks.

Responsibilities that are written into your contract."

She frowned, confused. "I'm sorry…what responsibilities?"

"The American Music Awards after-party for one. An extremely important brand partnership for FV you've now damaged. Antonio was mortified. Then you blew off Pascal's fittings for the new collection. Which should have been your number one priority."

She bit her lip. *That* felt like a slap in the face, given how hard she'd worked for FV over the past year, killing herself to ensure its success. All the times she'd gone above and beyond her mandate to ensure a campaign received the visibility it needed to catch fire. But right now, she needed to choose her words carefully. "I was so exhausted the night of the AMA party I could barely stand up. I had to be in Tokyo for a show the next day. I skipped the party, yes, but I did the awards as per my contract, a photo of which made it to the front page of the *New York Times*. As for Pascal's fittings," she concluded, "we only pushed them a few days."

"Days we do not have with a print and television campaign waiting in the wings. The most expensive in the company's history…in the *industry's* history. There is no room for error here,

Ms. Davis, something you don't seem to understand."

She absorbed his impenetrable expression. How immovable he was. "I have other commitments I need to meet, Cristiano. We all need to be flexible here."

His expression darkened into combustible blue fire. "We are five weeks away from the launch of Pascal's collection—a collection the world will be watching. The campaign for which has not yet been finished. *You* are the face of the FV brand—a job I am paying you twenty million dollars a year for. The largest contract of its kind in the business right now. There *are* no other priorities."

She absorbed the fury coming off of him. She got it—she did. She hadn't been prioritizing her FV work of late as much as she should have been. But what could she do? She'd been fighting the impossibility of her schedule for months, a schedule Tatiana had jam-packed, because her agent had made it clear she needed to make hay while the sun shone. Who knew how long she'd be on top? And quite frankly, she needed the money if her mother was to keep her house in Beverly Hills. But, she conceded, the impossibility of it all weighting her limbs, she also needed to keep Francesco Vitale—her marquee client—happy.

"I will talk to Tatiana," she offered in her most conciliatory voice. "We'll come up with a plan."

"Actually, I already have a plan," he dismissed, "one that will extricate us from this mess you've landed us in." He tipped his glass at her, the dark amber liquid glinting in the light. "My PR department has developed a strategy to rehabilitate your image. To do *damage control*. A couple of FV-sponsored charitable events over the next couple of weeks with a global reach that will cast you in a better light. Something for the press to feast on rather than their current diet."

"That's not going to knock them off course," Jensen protested. "It would be naive to think so. It would be better to let this die out like it undoubtedly will." *Eventually.* "And, besides," she tacked on, "I really don't think I can pack anything more into the next couple of weeks. I have multiple assignments to do before I fly to Milan, then a shoot in Cannes, the—"

He waved a hand at her, cutting her off. "Your agent is going to cancel those so you can focus on FV."

Her jaw dropped. *What? Tatiana was doing what?*

She couldn't possibly cancel those assignments. One of them was a show she was headlining in Shanghai for one of her favorite lingerie clients. Not to mention key assignments in Berlin and Cannes—one of them for an up-and-coming swimsuit brand she'd just signed on with. Business she needed to keep.

"That isn't possible," she said in as calm a voice as she could manufacture. "My clients are depending on me. They can't possibly replace me this late in the game."

"Clearly they will have to. You are the one blowing off the assignments, not me." He forged on, as if he hadn't just thrown a grenade at her. "The rest of the plan," he expanded, "is that you will travel back to Milan with me tonight. You will stay on my Lake Como estate where we are shooting the collection, out of the media eye, a level of discretion my security team will ensure. There will not be one more photograph, one more stunt, one more *indiscretion* before this launch, or I will personally cancel your contract so fast it will make your head spin."

Her stomach plunged to the floor. *She couldn't believe he was doing this*. Her rational brain told her he couldn't do it—that he would never do it given everything he'd invested in her. She *was* the brand right now. But another part of her was afraid he would. That challenging Cristiano Vitale in this moment would be a bad idea given the ruthless business-focused decisions he'd been making of late. Another of those career-limiting moves she didn't want to consider.

She set her gaze on his, eyes beseeching. "This isn't necessary. The headlines will stop, Cristiano, I promise. I can make it all work."

"It's already done." His gaze glinted, hard like polished sapphire. "This is the deal, Ms. Davis. Take it or leave it. I would advise," he suggested, a warning note in his voice, "you think very carefully before you reply. Because if you imagine I am bluffing, I can assure you that I am not. You are at the heart of my campaign. At the heart of the brand. I will do whatever I need to do to make sure you are in some kind of reasonable shape to deliver on everything you've promised. Trust me on this."

She stared at him, dismay sinking through her. He had just thrown the one thing at her she couldn't afford to lose—the contract she'd worked her entire career for. Not to mention the knock to her reputation she would suffer if she did lose it, a stain on her track record she could never erase. And then there was the fact that her powerful New York agent had apparently already weighed in—a decision she wished desperately she'd consulted her on. Which left her with no options.

"I clearly have no choice," she said evenly, meeting Cristiano Vitale's vibrant blue gaze.

"No," he said matter-of-factly, "you don't. We leave in an hour. Do what you need to do."

CHAPTER TWO

JENSEN WATCHED THE twinkling lights of London disappear as the sleek, luxurious jet climbed high into the night sky, rendering the world below a miniaturized replica of itself. Her head was still spinning from the events of the night, her equilibrium not so easily restored as the tiny jet had achieved in its quick climb above the clouds. *Freaking out* more accurately described her current state of mind.

They had stayed at the party long enough to make the perfunctory rounds and engage in the requisite small talk she'd needed to do on behalf of her clients, before they'd left via the back exit of the venue, thereby avoiding the throngs of press at the front. From there, they'd made a quick stop at her hotel to retrieve her things before continuing on to Luton airport, where they were to fly out of.

It had all happened with the rapid-fire efficiency the FV CEO was clearly used to. Cristiano had spent the entire ride to the airport on a call with Brazil, Portuguese rolling off his tongue as if it were his mother language, followed by a conversation with someone in LA, in which he'd plowed through a list of issues the subsidiary was facing with a razor-sharp intelligence and problem-solving ability that left her dizzy. When he'd closed off a conversation with China with a few sentences of fluent Mandarin, she'd observed the exchange with disbelief. Was there any language the man didn't speak?

She would have been impressed if she weren't consumed by the repercussions of his autocratic behavior on her career, and her worry about the impact it would have. She'd called Tatiana from the airport, searching for solutions. But her agent had simply restated the facts at hand. Cristiano Vitale was not happy with her recent headlines. He was her largest client and she had to keep him happy. End of story.

"Do whatever he wants for the next five weeks," her agent had advised, "until the launch. I'll deal with the rest."

Except this was her career. *Her* reputation. Her agent could likely reschedule the shoots she had planned, but Shanghai was another story. She either walked in the show or she forfeited the job to someone else. Not an option when she'd worked so hard to land the assignment.

When *reputation,* as her agent was so fond of saying, was everything in this business.

Her chest clenched, her fingers tightening around the mug of tea she held. Her career had always been her anchor—the one thing that had protected her when things fell apart, as they inevitably did in her life. She could not, *would not,* put that in jeopardy. Which meant she had to convince Cristiano she could manage all of this without him resorting to such drastic measures.

Her gaze bounced across the table, to where he sat opposite her in the luxuriously appointed seating area. Eyes on his laptop, his concentration complete, he looked formidably unapproachable, having stripped off his dark suit jacket to reveal the dove-white shirt, shirtsleeves pushed up to expose corded, muscular forearms. An impressive display that didn't end with those amazing arms, the fine material of his dark suit trousers emphasizing the equally powerful muscles of his thighs.

As intimidating as Millie had pegged him to be, he was also undeniably gorgeous, what was more than a five o'clock shadow darkening his lean cheeks, his generous, sensual mouth softening the impossibly hard lines of his face. And then there were those eyes, the darkest, most vivid blue she'd ever seen. A woman could drown in those if she let herself and not ever want to call for help.

Good God, she thought, summoning her rationality as a wave of primal heat coursed through her. So he was *manly* in the way Millie had described, far more attractive than the whipcord-lean male models she worked with, who never did it for her. *This* was not the way to a clear head. To the strategic thinking she clearly needed to possess if she was going to talk her way out of this mess.

She eyed his recently filled coffee cup, searching for a way to break the ice. "You're not afraid that's going to keep you up all night?" she murmured.

He set the coffee cup down, those incredible blue eyes moving to hers. "We *are* going to be up half the night. I might as well be productive with my time."

A state of affairs he clearly interpreted as her fault, she absorbed, surveying the faint traces of irritation creasing the edges of his mouth. He was still furious with her, that was obvious. It had been there in the brusque way he'd treated her ever since they'd left the party, using the minimum number of words necessary to communicate. A wall she needed to get past if she was going to right-side the situation.

"I apologize about the press," she said quietly.

"I know this is not the type of coverage you are looking for, Cristiano. But I promise you, there is very little truth to any of it. It's all been exaggerated way out of proportion. It will blow over before long, I'm sure of it."

"You think so?" He picked up a stack of paper and tossed it on the table in front of her. "My evening press clips. *Gaining* steam is more how I'd describe it."

She scanned the headline of the story on top.

Palace Readying a Statement to Deny Playboy Alexandre's Wild Love Life

Read on, through the first paragraph, which detailed an inside source at the palace who'd revealed the royal family would ask for the prince's privacy as he and Juliana "worked through their relationship." The same source who referred to her as a "diversion" for the prince, who couldn't possibly be taken seriously.

That hurt. Her stomach plunged, lodging itself somewhere above her twisting insides. But more than that, it was *ridiculous*. This had gotten out of hand. Completely out of hand. She flipped through the articles beneath, each more ludicrous than the last, earmarking her as the catalyst for the destruction of the rumored royal match. Jensen Davis, modern-day Scarlet Woman. *Man-wrecker extraordinaire*. The woman who would bring the royals down.

She bit her lip, tasting the salty tang of blood. This had gone far enough. She was through being the fall guy for her mother and Alexandre. Not when it came at the expense of her career. Her *reputation*.

She set her cup down and sat up straight, squaring her shoulders, her eyes on Cristiano. "I am not having an affair with Alexandre Santeval. He is a good friend of mine. The episode in the fountain was a stunt for my mother's show—one Alexandre went along with because he and Juliana had gotten into a fight and he wanted to make her jealous. I had no idea that he was going to take it this far. If I had, I never would have done it."

A skeptical look crossed his face. "So this is all the prince's fault?"

"No," she conceded, her chin dipping. "It was mine as well. I agreed to do the stunt. I bear responsibility for it, too."

His expression darkened. "And it didn't strike you as being *unwise*, given your current commitments? That this type of juvenile schoolyard stunt was a bad idea?"

She swallowed past the bitter taste of regret that stained her mouth. Yes, it *had* occurred to her that it was a bad idea. She'd signed off those stupid stunts when she'd left her mother's show. But she couldn't go that far with the truth. Not without revealing her mother's business, something Veronica Davis would never forgive her for.

She sank her teeth deeper into her lip. Eyed him. "I was exhausted. I don't always make the best decisions when I'm in that state of mind. Clearly," she acknowledged, for good measure, "this was not a good one."

Cristiano regarded her for a long moment, as if he was debating whether or not to believe her. She thought maybe he'd decided it was inconsequential when he finally spoke. "Good thing, then, that we have cleared your schedule and you will now be able to get some rest in Milan. Perhaps it will improve your decision-making skills."

Frustration bubbled up inside her. He was *impossible*. Not budging at all. "Tatiana," she elaborated, "thinks she can reschedule the shoots I have planned. But Shanghai is a live show—one I'm headlining. I was looking at this," she said, picking up the PR plan he'd handed her in the car. "There's no reason why I can't do Shanghai and keep my FV commitments. It's only one day."

"It's not one day," he replied, a hard edge to his voice. "It's two days of travel at a minimum, then the day of the show. Which will leave you jet-lagged and exhausted—the exact opposite of what all this is meant to accomplish. To allow you to focus on your FV work the way you should be. Not to mention the strategy of removing you from the media eye—perhaps my stronger reasoning at the moment."

She eyed the impenetrable terrain of his face. "Cristiano," she murmured, letting her dark lashes flutter down over her eyes in a gesture that always, without fail worked. "I understand that you are angry. I have apologized more than once for my actions. But I cannot miss this show. If I do, my reputation will suffer. Imagine if this were me, reneging on a million-dollar show with FV. How would you feel?"

"Furious," he agreed evenly. "Exactly as I do right now, given you've thrown my entire advertising schedule into chaos." He arched a dark brow at her. "Perhaps the better question is why you keep doing this to yourself. I've seen your schedule… Tatiana reviewed it with me. You would have to be superhuman to pull that off. *I* have a crazy schedule and it far supersedes mine. And for what?" he asked, flicking an elegant, Rolex-clad wrist at her. "So that you can host the entire French Riviera at one of your wild parties?"

Ooh. A bolt of heat moved through her. She was going to kill her mother. She truly was. She hiked her jaw higher. "That was a onetime thing. And the reason I work so hard is not to party, it's to protect myself. A top model only has a few years at her peak, then it's downhill from there. It's only smart business sense to maximize my earning potential."

"While you neglect your responsibilities and put those relationships in jeopardy?" He shook his head, an infuriated look on his face. "If you are so intent on protecting your career, I suggest you get a handle on your schedule. Rethink your current trajectory. Draw some lines between your personal and professional lives. Because I didn't sign up to put a Davis on my payroll. I signed up for the model with the power to transform my brand. *That's* what I want from you over the next few weeks."

A feeling of complete impotence swept over her. She'd attempted to do exactly that when she'd finally walked away from the show—to *not* be a Davis anymore. She'd spent her entire life at the mercy of the show and its scripted plotlines with utterly no power of her own. Yet now, when she'd finally cut those ties, her mother was still pulling her puppet strings from afar, to the detriment of everything Jensen held dear.

Her nails dug into her palms. *This* was the last time she allowed her to do it. The queen of manipulation was no longer going to orchestrate her life, no matter what sob story she threw at her. But first, she acknowledged, she needed to clean up the mess her mother had created. *Again.*

"You know what I've done for the brand," she said quietly, her eyes fixed on his. "That I've made it hip again. *Buzz-worthy.* That I've gone above and beyond the call of duty to do so. You might consider cutting me some slack."

"Give me a reason to do so," he returned in a voice hard as flint, "and I might consider it."

Cristiano observed Jensen as she curled up in the chair opposite him, an embattled look on her beautiful face. She had batted those long, dark lashes at him, fully expecting him to capitulate—the usual reaction she undoubtedly elicited from men—and allow her to jet halfway across the world to China, as if he hadn't already made it clear what her responsibilities were for the next five weeks. How *unhappy* he was with the current situation.

She had chutzpah, that was for certain. And maybe, he conceded, eyeing those luminous dark eyes and impossibly long lashes, she'd had reason to believe it could have worked. He'd have to have been deaf, dumb and blind not to admit she was beautiful. It had been there in that initial flash of attraction between them at the party tonight.

His gaze slid over her, curled up in the seat. She'd removed the dramatic stage makeup she'd been wearing. Without it, she looked about eighteen rather than twenty-six, her high cheekbones and full mouth set off by a flawless honey-hued complexion that made makeup unnecessary. And then there was the perfect voluptuous body beneath the silky material of the soft white T-shirt and black yoga pants she wore. The long legs that went on forever.

He would have to be far less of the man that he was not to imagine them wrapped around him in a hot, no-holds-barred encounter. She'd sold that particular fantasy the first time he'd ever laid eyes on her in that shoot. It was why he'd hired her—because he'd wanted to wrap that all-American sex appeal around his brand. Which didn't mean he was going to allow her to play him like she'd clearly done so many others.

He studied the shadows beneath those glittering, dark eyes. One minute she was the brilliant businesswoman he'd seen flashes of, the next the wild child the papers liked to capture her as. And then, there were those glimpses of vulnerability he swore he saw, so fleeting they were there one minute and gone the next.

What must it have been like to grow up as

a Davis? In front of America, with your entire life on display? With no buffer from the world. He couldn't actually imagine, given the strict, traditional upbringing he'd had. Perhaps it explained her inability to make good decisions. Not helped by the fact that she'd had two of the greatest stars Hollywood had ever known as parents, notoriously emotional, dramatic personalities who couldn't have made good role models.

Which was all inconsequential, he reminded himself. Even if she hadn't engaged in a very public affair with Alexandre Santeval, she'd still gone along with the stunt, recklessly putting her reputation and the reputation of his brand at risk. Not an option, when he'd spent his entire career at FV attempting to pull his legacy out of the ashes and restore it to its former glory. When his grandfather, who had been both mentor and father to him after he and his sister Ilaria had lost their parents in a boating accident as teenagers, had entrusted him with the future of an Italian legend. When not one piece of his plan to reinvent FV could go wrong without the whole thing tumbling down around him like a house of cards. A pressure he went to bed with every night and woke to every morning.

He set his gaze on the woman opposite him, her dark eyes fixed on the night sky beyond the window. She was on some kind of a spiral—one he was determined to put an end to using whatever methods he deemed necessary. Because there was no way he was going to let her run helter-skelter through his life, causing more of that particular brand of mayhem she engendered. Not with everything he'd built coming to fruition at this very moment, a crucial few weeks in which he couldn't afford to take his eyes off the ball.

She was clearly incapable of taking care of herself. So he was going to have to do it for her. Even if it killed him in the process.

He worked through the next couple of hours before they landed in Milan. Jensen slept through most of the flight, waking up for the transfer to the helicopter that would fly them up to Lake Como before promptly falling asleep again, a Herculean effort given the noise in the aircraft. He let her sleep, because it looked like she hadn't done so in weeks, waking her when they approached Villa Barberini, situated on a hill above the western shore of the lake.

Magnificent in the late-night hour, the lights from the estate spilled out onto the dark, silent water. Built by an Italian count who'd constructed the spectacular thirty-thousand-square-foot showpiece to entertain his many famous guests, it sprawled across the hill from high up in the village of Moltrasio all the way down to the lake's shore.

Constructed of thick layers of ancient stone, the elegant cream-stuccoed villa was surrounded by magnificent gardens preserved exactly as they had been centuries ago, olive trees flourishing alongside ancient date palms and lemon trees. But most sensational of all was the view of the lake and the mountains from every vantage point on the property.

Jensen blinked in the light, rubbing her eyes with her fists. "I must look a sight."

Cristiano eyed the full curve of her mouth, pillowy soft in the filtered light. The darkness of her sleep-softened eyes, her chestnut-colored hair spilling over her shoulders in a tumbled, silken swath. She looked exactly like the type of woman a man would want to wake up to in his bed. In an albeit spectacular fantasy. Although sleep, he conceded, a series of carnal images flashing through his head, would be the last thing on his mind.

His gaze met hers in the dim light, and he was fairly sure he hadn't wiped the erotic images out of his head fast enough, her dark eyes widening as a current of electricity passed between them. It hung there, pulsing on the air in the intimate confines of the space, until his pilot broke the silence, announcing his intention to land.

"You look fine," he murmured, a rough note to his voice. "You should buckle up."

Jensen nodded, ripped her gaze from his and fumbled with the belt around her waist. When her awkward attempts to tighten it proved fruitless in the thick tension between them, he reached over and did it himself, inhaling the tantalizing scent of her perfume as he did.

She was some kind of sorceress, he thought, as the helicopter set itself down on the landing pad near the main house, whipping up the wind in the silver-leafed olive trees. Because no way was this logical thinking. It had clearly been too long since he'd slept himself.

Once it was safely on the ground, he jumped out of the helicopter, its blades still whirring a slowing pattern. Wary about Jensen's ability to navigate the step in the darkness given her fatigue and half-asleep state, he caught her, hands around her waist, and lowered her to the ground when she misjudged the depth of the step, a smothered sound of surprise leaving her lips as she pitched forward.

"Sorry," she breathed, the warmth of her breath skating across his cheek. "I got a bit dizzy. I haven't slept much the past few days."

His hand splayed across her bottom, holding her securely. He didn't let go immediately, afraid from the way she swayed she didn't quite have her legs underneath her. The intimate fit of her lush curves against the hard length of him did something strange to his senses. Heated his blood in a way he hadn't felt in ages. And suddenly, those erotic images he'd envisioned waking up to replayed themselves in his head in vivid Technicolor detail. Except this time, he knew what she felt like, and he wasn't certain it was an image he could get out of his head.

Which was *folle*, he breathed, because she was trouble, and this was the last thing he should be thinking. Moving his hand up to a more respectable position at her waist, he set her away from him. That inconvenient chemistry flared between them, dark eyes fixed on blue, smoking up the air between them for a long, infinitesimal second, before she slicked her tongue over her lips in a nervous movement and stepped back, his arm dropping away from her waist.

"Thank you," she murmured in a husky voice. "That could have been a nasty fall."

He doused the heat snaking through his body with a superhuman effort, because *this* was not happening between them. *He* was here to enforce the rules. Nothing more.

"The last thing I need is you walking down the runway in a cast. It would be bad for business." He picked up her bag along with his own, ignored the way her jaw had dropped open and carried it toward the house, where he introduced her to his housekeeper, Filomena, who had waited up for them. Introductions complete, he sent Filomena off to bed, then showed Jensen the way down the lamplit path toward her accommodations.

Located within walking distance of the main house, the small dwelling sat directly across the vibrant blue depths of a spotlit butterfly-shaped pool, fed by a waterfall that cascaded softly into the far end. Constructed of floor-to-ceiling windows that maximized the view and fully equipped with everything she would need for a multi-week stay, lamplight poured from the windows onto the sparkling surface of the water.

"The pool house," Jensen murmured, surveying its proximity to the main villa. "You truly do mean to babysit me, don't you?"

"Si," he murmured, "You've driven me to it."

She cocked a brow at him. "Aren't you afraid I'll cramp your style? What if you have a hot date?"

"I will manage." He set her bag down on the porch and propped himself up against one of the pillars, which rose gracefully to the roof. "Here are the rules. You will remain on this property, where you will carry out whatever task my marketing team requires of you, which includes following through on the PR plan in its entirety. Someone will be by to brief you on it in the morning. Filomena will be at your disposal for anything you require while you're here. Simply ask her, and it will be done."

"Where is the rest of the crew staying?"

"In the cottages near the lake. If you have free time," he continued, "you are welcome to use any of the facilities on the estate. If you swim, however, please notify a member of the staff so they can keep an eye on you. And," he added with emphasis, "if you could keep your clothes on, it would be much appreciated. For the staff's sake."

And for his, to be honest.

Her full mouth twisted. "I will do my best. Sometimes I just find myself with the *need* to disrobe. I can't always catch myself before it happens."

He eyed the dark glitter in her eyes. She was baiting him. And while a part of him would love to pursue it, considering the Y chromosomes he possessed, another more sensible part of him recognized it for the folly it was. He found nothing about the fountain episode amusing, nor should she, given that *Hollywood Divas* had been fined in excess of a quarter of a million euros for the episode, which had left all Italians unamused. Although he suspected it had been more than worth it from the show's perspective, given the massive ratings it had engendered.

"Make yourself at home," he said, shutting down that very male part of his brain. "Invite a friend or two over. You are free to leave the estate to do an errand, provided you have Saul, my bodyguard, with you. He will make sure you are protected from the photographers. You will not," he underscored, "under any circumstance, throw any parties on the estate or use any illegal drugs. Nor will you go clubbing or undertake any other activity that will put you in the limelight, unless it is specifically outlined in the PR plan. When I said no headlines, I meant *no* headlines." He set a hard gaze on her. *"Capisci?"*

She eyed him. "I don't take drugs."

"I know the scene, Jensen. It's full of them."

"Not with me. *Ever.* It's the quickest way for a model to ruin her looks."

He thought she might be telling the truth, because her dark, lustrous eyes were clear, her thick, wavy hair, the color of darkest cocoa, lustrous, as was the unmarred expanse of perfect, sun-kissed skin that covered every inch of her. Which only brought to mind what she'd look like with nothing on at all.

"Bene," he murmured, refusing to let his mind wander. "Then it won't be a problem."

She crossed her arms over her chest and leaned back against the railing. "What about Pascal and the fittings? Will I travel to FV for those?"

"Pascal is going to come here and do them, starting tomorrow afternoon. It will save him moving the clothing back and forth for the shoot. Which begins on Wednesday," he qualified, "followed by the television commercial, which they expect will take a few days to shoot. We are cutting it close on all of it, so make sure you get some rest. It's going to be a busy few weeks."

Her lips firmed, and he got the impression she barely resisted rolling her eyes. "I'm used to that," she murmured. "Is there anything else you'd like to decree, while you're so clearly on a roll? Anything else that would keep you happy?"

"Si," he returned in a soft, unmistakably commanding tone. "What I would *like* is to hear from my staff that you are going above and beyond to accommodate their needs. That their stress levels have been greatly reduced over the next few days. And *then*, I will be happy."

Fiery dark eyes rested on his, but she wisely abstained from perpetuating this battle between them further. He pushed away from the wall, intent on getting some sleep, before the lack of it made him partake in any other irrational thoughts that were wholly unwise.

"*Buona notte*, Jensen. Get some sleep. You're going to need it."

CHAPTER THREE

"SANTO CIELO. You've lost at least ten pounds… What have you been doing? Not eating at all?"

Jensen stood completely still as Pascal Ferrari stuck yet another pin into the midnight-blue gown she was wearing, a dark frown on his expressive face. She knew she'd lost weight. She'd been too stressed and working too much over the past few weeks to eat proper meals, which was revealing itself in the gaping fabric at the back of the dress. A state of affairs that had, unfortunately, meant that quite a few pieces of Pascal's collection had required alteration, not ideal at this stage of the game.

"Mi dispiace," she murmured, flashing him a guilty look. *I'm sorry.* "My schedule has been nuts. I'm too tired to eat when I get home, I have breakfast, and then it starts all over again."

"I guess," the designer exhaled on a pained breath as he affixed yet another pin to the dress, "I should be grateful you didn't blow in at the eleventh hour, expecting me to fix it. I had visions of a week spent pulling the shoot out of the fire."

Jensen sank her teeth into her lip. Absorbed the strain written across Pascal's charismatic features. He'd nearly wept with relief when she'd appeared for the fittings, his happiness at finding a break in her schedule palpable. Which had made her feel awful. He had the weight of the world on his shoulders with his first collection as the new design chief of FV set to debut in weeks. The shoes he had to fill in Francesco's as big as they got. But she'd been too overbooked and overwhelmed to even consider what this must have been doing to him—one of her absolute favorite designers. The pressure it had put him under. So she'd tried to make it up to him the best way she could.

When they hadn't been shooting the collection in gorgeous lakeside locations on the Vitale estate, they'd been finalizing the lineup piece by piece so it would be perfect for the shoot and show. Which had every muscle and bone in her body aching from the interminably long days spent in front of the camera, followed by these sessions with Pascal.

It had gone some way toward assuaging the guilt she'd felt toward shirking her duties. But it was doing little to alleviate the anxiety eating away at her insides when it came to her career. Tatiana had managed to reschedule her shoot in Paris, but Berlin had to go ahead without her, and Cannes, an assignment for an up-and-coming swimsuit brand, was still a question mark, given the date couldn't be altered and her client didn't want anyone else. Not helped by the fact that her American lingerie client had hired Ariana Lordes, a Brazilian superstar in the making, to take her place headlining the show in Shanghai—a highly visible replacement that had everyone talking.

It was unnerving to lose the job, given how hard she'd worked for it. The buzz about Ariana was immense, and she couldn't help but feel insecure. What if her client, who hadn't been happy at all with her last-minute cancellation, loved Ariana? What if they decided they liked her *better*? Not helped by all the rumor and innuendo over why she'd been replaced, which she hadn't been able to comment on at all.

The only thing she knew for sure was that in the cutthroat, fast-paced world of high fashion modeling, there was always another girl waiting in the wings, ready to take her place, a prospect that had left her with an ever-present knot in her stomach. So she'd decided to do the only thing she could do: throw herself into her work and focus on the things she *could* control—a tactic that was working with limited effect.

"I'm sorry I've been MIA," she told Pascal as he finished with the back of the dress and sat back on his heels to peruse his work. "I've been trying to do too much. I'll do better."

He waved a hand at her. "You're the world's top model. You are busy. *In demand.* Would I like to have more of you? Of course. But you are a consummate professional when I do have you, and you make magic with my dresses. That's what matters."

"I'm not so sure Cristiano would agree," she said drily. "He's not very happy with me."

He shrugged a shoulder. "Cristiano is under a great deal of pressure right now. He's spent the last eighteen months battling his grandfather and then the board on the way forward. Digging the company out of the dark ages. He's taken a big risk on me. Not to mention having the weight of a national legacy resting on his shoulders."

She was intrigued. "What did Cristiano and Francesco disagree about?"

A wry smile curved his mouth. "What *didn't* they butt heads about? Francesco was old-school. He didn't get the new realities. How the fashion world has changed. The markets we need to capture if this company is to survive."

He waved a hand at her. "Look at his opinion of you. He didn't value you as the influencer that you are because he didn't understand the current social climate. Cristiano does."

She absorbed the additional perspective. It was the reason she'd signed on with FV, a brand many would have called a fading star. Because she'd believed in the company's current direction. In Cristiano's plans. In his track record as a brilliant thinker and marketer. But she'd always sensed that Francesco, whom she'd worked closely with until his death three months prior, had not been a fan of hers—an opinion she hadn't seemed able to shake.

"And then there was Francesco and me," Pascal continued, a mischievous sparkle in his dark eyes. "We were just as bad. We rattled the rafters some days."

She frowned. "What did you two disagree about? Francesco chose you as his heir apparent, after all."

He threw up an expressive hand. "Francesco was a rose and I am a garden bursting with outrageous color. He had his vision, I had mine. I knew it would be fine when I eventually took over. Meanwhile," he conceded, his wry smile deepening, "Cristiano had to play referee, which couldn't have been easy for him."

Which, in hindsight, made Cristiano's actions

more understandable. His autocratic behavior with her had been infuriating, but she could see, given the pressure he was under, why he might have done it. She had backed him into a corner. Given him no choice. Not that it made what he'd done okay. She was still intent on convincing him to allow her to do Cannes, once she'd demonstrated to him he had nothing to worry about. That she would do her job. She intended to knock his socks off.

As for that strange, inexplicable attraction she'd sensed between them the night they'd arrived? Her mind went back to the moment he'd lifted her down from the helicopter. The heat that had pulsed between them. She would almost have believed she'd imagined it she'd been so exhausted, practically hallucinating by the time her face hit the gazillion-thread-count pillow. Except it had been too palpable, too *real* for her to have conjured it up.

The sensation of his tall, hard body plastered against hers was still imprinted in her head. The spicy, intoxicating male scent of him. It didn't take much for her to imagine him without the clothes in an intimate encounter of another kind. How impressive he would look. Which was insane thinking, because just as he'd clearly turned it off that night, it was ridiculous to even think about it.

He thought her *beneath* him. That was clear. A royal pain in his behind. She would do well to put it out of her head and concentrate on what was important here. Impressing him with her work, so she could get back to her other assignments and undo the dents she'd done to her career.

She looked down as a message buzzed on her phone, sitting on the table. *Her mother.* If a silver lining existed in all of this, it was that here, on Cristiano's fortress of an estate, her mother couldn't get to her. Not that she hadn't tried. She'd called, shortly after Jensen had arrived in Milan, over the moon with the royal buzz. Had proposed a follow-up stunt to the Alexandre story to keep the buzz going for next season. Jensen had told her no, absolutely not. And this time, she'd meant it. She was staying on Cristiano's estate and immersing herself in her work, she'd told her mother, which she desperately needed at the moment.

When Veronica Davis had responded to the whole idea of her staying on Cristiano's exclusive estate with the glee of a genie rubbing her hands together, calling him "beyond delicious" with that Machiavellian brain of hers, Jensen had stopped her in her tracks. Made it clear that Cristiano and her FV work were off-limits, not to be touched under any circumstance. Which didn't mean her mother had listened to her, a worry that percolated in the back of her head. But given that was another of those things she had no control over, all she could do was try to make her mother see how serious she was about it, the part of this she *could* control.

She reached down and swiped the message from the screen without reading it. She was done with her mother. The only thing she planned on doing this evening, given she and Pascal were finishing early for once, was to keep her date with the hot tub outside the pool house, its views of the lake legendary. Which might go some way toward easing some of the wickedly sore muscles in her body so she could actually work tomorrow.

She had just stepped out onto the terrace on a hot, sultry night in Moltrasio, intent on a light dinner and an early night after her epic soak in the Jacuzzi, when a shadow fell over the gray stone tile. She looked up, a smile on her face, expecting it to be Filomena who normally stopped by with news of dinner at around this time. Instead, she found herself face-to-face with Cristiano, dressed in dark jeans and a blue T-shirt, his jet-black hair scraped back from his face as if freshly wet from the shower. The designer jeans hugging the powerful muscles of his thighs, the T-shirt defining the impressive line of his abs, dark stubble shading his jaw, he was blatantly male in a way that stole her breath.

Caught off guard, she pressed the book she'd been about to read to her chest, drawing his attention to the flirty neckline of the rose-colored sundress she wore. Which exposed nothing really, except for an expanse of tanned skin and bare shoulders, yet she somehow felt branded by his dark appraisal, which moved slowly over her, missing nothing.

"Checking up on me?" she murmured, to divert her attention from the warm burst of awareness that moved through her. "Making sure I'm not off lighting up the town? Causing a ruckus? Because I can assure you the only plans I have for this evening are a glass of wine and this book. Very exciting, I know."

His hard mouth quirked. "Actually," he drawled, his rich, lightly accented voice sending a shiver of response through her, "I hear you've been working hard. I thought that since I'm home early tonight, we could have dinner together. Talk about the upcoming week. We have some engagements we are doing together it would be good to discuss. Filomena has prepared a fantastic linguine carbonara. I can promise an equally good bottle of wine to go with it."

Have dinner with him? She eyed him silently.

He wasn't wearing that combustive look anymore. He looked relaxed and almost approachable. Amiable, even. Was this a peace offering? And if so, would it be wise for her to reject it?

She chewed on her lip. Could one dinner hurt? Surely she could suffer his infuriating arrogance for an hour or so? Ignore how he looked in jeans and a T-shirt, which took his level of attractiveness from superior to somewhere approaching drool-worthy.

"All right," she agreed, "that would be lovely. Where will we eat?"

"On the main terrace." He tipped his head in the direction of the house. "Shall we?"

She deposited her book on the table beside the lounger and fell into step beside him on the stone path. Even at five foot nine, she was dwarfed by him, the warm palm he held to her back large and masculine, sinking into her skin and warming her all the way through.

She got the distinct impression that, despite his autocratic behavior, he was at his core a gentleman. An opinion that was confirmed when he pulled out her chair for her on the torchlit patio and ensured she was seated before he sat down opposite her. Resplendent with a glorious mix of primary colors that spilled from the flowerpots and shrubs along its periphery, the terrace offered a magnificent view of the glittering, cerulean-blue lake, bathed in a golden pink shimmer as the sun sank below the mountains.

It was a ridiculously romantic setting. Although clearly this was a business dinner, and Cristiano was merely keeping tabs on her, just as he'd promised he would do. Still, it was hard not to enjoy the spectacular setting and the even better Chianti Filomena poured for them both, its fruity, full-bodied flavor exactly what she needed after a ridiculously long day that had begun at the crack of dawn.

They traded small talk about how the shoot was going, presided over by one of the world's top fashion photographers, and the social media posts she'd been doing to tease the campaign. Cristiano was an excellent conversationalist, sharing some of his own plans for the company, smart, strategic ideas that revealed more of that razor-sharp brain of his.

Sprawled in the chair opposite her, the hard, angular bones of his face powerful and perfectly put together in the candlelight, his effortless charisma was so imposingly male it was impossible not to be aware of him on a physical level. To wonder what it would be like to be on a real date with him, with all of that intensity focused on her with an end goal of an entirely different nature. Which made her glad for the small talk they exchanged, so she could attempt to avoid that distracted thinking.

"Speaking of partnerships," he murmured, sitting back in his chair and cradling his wine-glass in his hand as Filomena cleared away the main course, "I met with Nicholas Zhang this afternoon."

Nicholas Zhang? Jensen knew Nicholas. Few would not. The consumer goods scion was one of the most powerful businessmen in Asia, his empire ranging from household goods to health products to fashion and beauty. It was why Cristiano would be talking to him, when he could be considered a competitor to FV, that intrigued her.

She arched a brow at him. "You are considering a partnership with him?"

He lifted his glass of wine to his mouth and took a sip. Savored it before he set the glass down. "He is buying a one-billion-dollar stake in Francesco Vitale."

Her eyes widened. FV had been a family-controlled company for fifty years—ever since Francesco had founded it as a young window dresser in Milan. It was a revered Italian fashion powerhouse. *Iconic.* The thought of Cristiano ceding any amount of control over it to a foreign entity seemed inconceivable. "Why?" she breathed.

"Because we don't have the financial ability to square off against the mega giants taking over the industry," he said, matter-of-factly. "This will allow us to do so. It will also offer us unparalleled access to the Asian market, which is critical to our success."

Which made complete sense. The fashion show she'd been slated to do in Shanghai had been for an American label. Everyone wanted to plunder the luxury fashion market, and Asia, with its massive growth opportunities, was the most coveted jewel in the crown. It was, however, a huge departure in strategy for the venerable Francesco Vitale, which had always prided itself on being *above* the industry. Untouchable in its prestige.

"That's a big move," she observed.

"Si," he agreed. "But necessary." He tipped his glass at her, his blue gaze intent. "I need you to do me a favor. Zhang mentioned to me that his sixteen-year-old daughter, Ming Li, is accompanying him to Milan next week. She wants to shop. Attend the Associazione Nazionale della Moda Italiana party with him. She is, in Zhang's words, *obsessed* with you. I thought you could dress her for the party. Take her under your wing. Show her a good time. Within reason," he qualified, with a pointed look. "She does not need to be learning bad behavior from

you, although I'm sure you can teach her that in abundance."

She ignored the slight and gave him an intrigued look. "So, you need my *help*."

"Si." He looked a bit pained as the word crossed his lips. Sensuous, beautiful lips it was hard to keep her eyes off of.

Her head flicked to Cannes, looming less than three weeks away—a pressing issue that had yet to be resolved. "What do I get in return?"

"A gold star for good behavior." He said it with a completely deadpan expression. "You are due a few of those, don't you think?"

"I thought I already had a whole scrapbook full of them with all of the work I've done to build the brand." She eyed him in the candlelight. "You do realize I did an entire behind-the-scenes video at the spring launch that has garnered millions of views? That the press office has been besieged with phone calls about the dress I wore to the AMAs, with people wanting to buy it before it's even out? That I've done double the amount of social media posts I'm contracted to do on behalf of FV in order to ensure the brand's success?"

"I had not realized all of that, no," he murmured. "It is much appreciated, however."

She toyed with the stem of her glass. Decided

this was her opportunity to get through to him. "This partnership isn't just a business deal to me, Cristiano. I've loved the brand ever since I was a teenager." A whimsical smile touched her lips. "My mother used to wear Francesco's designs, back in the day, when she was doing pictures. They were elegant, *ethereal*. Sophisticated, yet romantic. I was obsessed with them. I used to play dress-up in them with my sisters. Once," she acknowledged, "I spilled grape juice on one of his couture pieces and my mother nearly blew a gasket. I lost my allowance for weeks. But it was worth it to me."

His hard mouth curved in a rather devastating smile. "So it was a goal to model for FV?"

"The *ultimate* goal. I knew I could help revive the brand. Return it to its former glory. I liked your plans—what you were doing with the company. I even went against my agent's advice to go with Denali instead, because I believed in the brand so much. But for me," she explained, "it's always been about my personal style. I couldn't just wear the FV pieces, I had to make them my own. So I styled them with my own fashion sense, made the look signature Jensen, which resonated with my followers. They've started to see the brand as current again. *Fashion forward*."

He inclined his head. "You have delivered on

your promises, I don't disagree. I am merely trying to make sure you continue to deliver on those promises in the way I am paying you to do."

She eyed him quietly. "It's been a rough few weeks, Cristiano. I admit it. There's no question about it. But I've worked my butt off for the brand, and will continue to do so to make this launch a success. And yes, I will help you with Ming Li. But in exchange, I need something from you."

He arched a brow. "Which is?"

"A deal," she murmured. "I help you win Nicholas Zhang and his daughter over, and you let me do my shoot in Cannes."

Cristiano sat back in his chair, observing Jensen from over the rim of his glass. She looked fairly angelic this evening dressed in a pastel-colored sundress, her dark hair caught up in a ponytail, her delicate face free of makeup, all of that sun-kissed skin on display. He'd be lying if he didn't admit he was drawn to her. That the vibrancy she exuded did something to him—kicked something alive in him that had long remained dormant. He'd found himself just as caught up in her as everyone else as he'd watched her work this week, making magic with the camera. But he was also aware that she was far from an angel. That she'd raised hell for his brand over the past few weeks, and he wasn't about to give her full rein so that she could do it again.

His gaze rested on the determined set of her lush, full mouth. She didn't give up. It was a quality he admired about her. He needed her, and she knew it. And quite frankly, given how hard she'd worked over the past few days, his staff full of nothing but compliments about her professionalism, along with the fact that he thought he might have been a bit quick to judge, given his anger, he was content to give a little here, particularly if she helped him with Ming Li.

"Bene," he replied. "Prove to me I can trust you over the next three weeks and you can do Cannes."

The tense, watchful lines of her face relaxed. *"Grazie.* I can assure you, you have nothing to worry about."

He wasn't entirely convinced on that point. The last thing he needed was her going off the rails again, particularly when he was involving her with Nicholas Zhang and his daughter— an opportunity he couldn't afford to pass up. Zhang was a cagey customer, a tough negotiator at the best of times, whose signature was far from guaranteed on the deal they were negotiating. Which meant he needed all the aces up his sleeve he could manage. Having Jensen—his resident wild card—mess this deal up for him was not an option. Which meant he needed to figure out what made her tick, given they were going to spend the next few weeks working at each other's side.

She had been reliable at the beginning of her contract, a true professional according to his marketing team. So what had caused her to go off the rails? If it wasn't Alexandre Santeval, which he tended to believe, nor a drug or alcohol habit, which he also believed was not the issue, what had spurred all the wild partying? The outrageous antics? Because she couldn't shake her legacy as a Davis? Because it was her natural inclination to act out? Or was it something else she wasn't sharing?

He thought back to an incident when he and his younger sister Ilaria had been in middle school, his grandparents their de facto parents after they had lost their own. A boy his age had stolen his sister's lunch and left her in tears. Cristiano had wanted to punch him in the face. His grandmother, however, had counseled him not to. Had said that whatever had made the boy steal his sister's lunch had been rooted in far more than mere malice. Which had turned out to be true—the boy's family struggling over a bitter divorce, which had ripped it apart. A boy Cristiano had later become friends with, his best friend Rafe.

The story lingering in his head, he sat back in his chair as Filomena poured their coffee, along with a traditional Italian Amaro, then disappeared back inside. "I do wonder," he said idly, his eyes on Jensen, "what's been going on the past few weeks? What's sent you into this spiral you seem to be on? Because, to your point, this behavior was not an issue over the first year of your contract. So perhaps you can share what it is. Maybe I can help."

Her dark eyes widened, an emotion he couldn't identify flitting across her face. She veiled it just as quickly, her long lashes sweeping down over her cheeks. "Nothing is going on," she said quietly. "I overextended myself. Made some bad decisions, just like I said."

"And the wild partying?"

"Is how the press paints it." She threw up a hand, her ebony eyes glittering in the candlelight. "I didn't stumble out of Zoro after the incident with Juliana, Cristiano. I *tripped* over the sidewalk, there were so many photographers chasing me. I rarely drink much when I go out for the same reason I don't do drugs— because it would mess with my looks. As far as Monaco goes, some of my...*friends* got a little out of hand that night. It was not ideal, I agree, and also my fault, because ultimately, it was my hotel suite. *My responsibility.* I am not, however," she said, her gaze meeting his, "on a spiral, as you put it. On the contrary, if anything, I've been working far too much, which is my biggest problem."

He scoured the frustrated set of her jaw. The very real emotion written across her face. She was either a very good liar, or she was telling the truth. For some reason, he tended to think it was the latter, which either made him a fool or right, that there was something else going on with her she wasn't sharing. Because this type of behavior didn't come out of nowhere. And given his instincts were usually accurate, he went with the second theory.

"Your agent should be managing these things for you," he pointed out. "It's what you pay her for. Tell her it's too much, that you need to cut back."

Her dark gaze slid away from his. "It's not that simple. People depend on me. *Clients* depend on me. I have a reputation to protect."

"Which will only benefit from you pulling back and taking stock." He waved a hand at her. "What's going to happen if you take a step back? Maybe take on a client or two less? Look at Shanghai. The world hasn't come to an end because you didn't walk in the show."

Her chin lifted. "Ariana Lordes took my place in Shanghai. She is a bona fide superstar. Everyone's talking about it."

He studied the vulnerability written across her face, a fascinating crack in the perfect armor. Remembered what she'd said on the plane about the short duration of a model's career. Her reluctance to give even a little on her insane schedule. "And so you worry that what?" he challenged. "She will take your place? That you will lose your relevance? You can't control what happens in the industry, Jensen. *No one* can control that. All you can do is make the best decisions for your career. For you. For what *you* need."

She was silent for a long moment, her ebony eyes contemplative. "Life is more complicated than that."

He wasn't content with that answer. "How so?"

"It just is." She caught her lip between her teeth. "My career is important to me, Cristiano. It's more than just a job. It's—"

"What?" he pressed, thinking he might finally be getting somewhere.

"It's my grounding force. It's the only solid thing I've ever had in my life. I will not put it in jeopardy."

That kicked him right in the chest. Thudded hard in his inner recesses. His gaze moved over the vibrant, beautiful lines of her face, the fragility he sensed about her in this moment so completely at odds with everything she'd thrown at him thus far.

What must it have been like to grow up like she had? In a world where nothing was real? Where the news value of what she was living ruled the day? Where the solid, grounding existence he'd experienced as a Vitale would never have been even remotely possible for her? How had she handled it? What impact had it had on her? His curiosity resurfaced, stronger than ever.

"What was it like?" he asked quietly. "To be a Davis? To grow up like that?"

She eyed him, an emotion he couldn't read flickering across her face. "That's a fairly broad question," she murmured. "We could be here all night."

"Humor me." He waved a hand at her. "You were on television from when you were very young to just recently, no?"

"From when I was ten to when I was twenty-three." She was silent for a long moment, swirling her wine in her glass, the ruby-red liquid glittering in the candlelight. "It was," she said finally, "the furthest thing from normal you could imagine. When other kids were climbing trees, my sisters and I were memorizing plot lines. We shot ten to twelve hours a day, so we couldn't go to school. We had tutors instead. And a nanny when I was younger. Everyone on the show had to sign an NDA, which meant I rarely got to spend time with my friends whose parents wanted nothing to do with the show. Which was most of them," she acknowledged, her mouth twisting. "I don't blame them at all."

So in essence, he concluded, his heart pulsing for the young girl she'd been, she hadn't *had* a childhood. He could identify, on some level, given he'd lost his own parents at fourteen, when the boat they'd been piloting had crashed head-on into another vessel, killing his father instantly, and his mother days after. He'd been shattered. Annihilated at the loss. But he'd had no choice but to grow up fast, to mourn his parents from a place deep inside, rather than reveal his grief to the world, to give in to it, because his younger sister had needed him.

They'd been lucky enough to be put into his grandparents' care, but in the years following his father's death, Francesco had been heartbroken. Consumed by his grief, his grandmother preoccupied in her efforts to comfort him. They had, however, had the traditional family structure his grandparents had provided for them.

The solid base to his life Jensen had never had. And for that, he would be eternally grateful.

"That couldn't have been easy," he observed. "Not having any kind of a normal life. How did you feel about it?" Because she'd always been positioned as the ringleader. The girl who would try anything.

She shrugged a slim shoulder. "In some ways, it was fun—a new adventure every day. We received a lot of attention…what teenage girl wouldn't like that? But then," she continued, a frown creasing her brow, "it all became a bit much in our teenage years. It never stopped. The show…the media coverage. We had no privacy. It was impossible to carry on a real relationship. So my sisters and I decided to get out. Ava and Scarlett started a fashion and design business in Manhattan, and I began modeling."

"Which made sense given your background as a fashion influencer." He tipped his coffee cup at her. "Was it an easy transition?"

Her mouth curved in a rueful smile. "Technically, yes. I had a natural fashion sense. I knew how to act, which is a crucial part of modelling. But few people in the business took me seriously in the beginning. I was an influencer, not a model. My celebrity, my built-in endorsement value, might have gained me access into the upper echelons of modeling, but it was also a strike against me. Brands were wary of hiring me. Other models were resentful when they did. I had to work twice as hard as everyone else to land jobs, and sometimes even that wasn't enough."

He recalled his own skepticism when she'd been presented to him as a candidate for the face of his brand. He'd pretty much dismissed the idea out of hand, based on her reputation alone, even after she'd established herself as a top model. Which was a perfect example of how hard it must have been for her to overcome that prejudice lobbied against her.

"But you persevered," he pointed out. "That took guts."

She shrugged. "It was the only thing I knew. I wasn't afraid of hard work. Of having to prove myself, and people eventually began to see that I was serious. That I was good at my job."

Only for her to put it all in jeopardy with this spiral she'd been on of late. It made no sense. Not when he could see how seriously she took her career. Which made him more mystified than ever.

He hiked a dark brow. "And so, you thought that by frolicking naked in the Trevi Fountain with a playboy prince and setting off an international scandal, it was going to preserve your stellar reputation?"

Her long, sooty lashes swept down to veil her gaze. "No," she said quietly, "I did not. Sometimes my…*impulses* get the better of me. Old habits die hard, I guess."

He eyed the wealth of emotion simmering behind those midnight-dark eyes. He wasn't getting the full truth here. He was getting partial truths. He was sure of it. He had the distinct feeling she'd just thrown him a line—told him what he'd wanted to hear—just to get him off the subject. And why that bothered him, why he wanted to get to the bottom of her, he didn't know.

He could tell himself it was because she was a crucial asset to him and he couldn't have her going sideways during this launch. But he thought it might be more. That there was something about that vulnerable light in her eyes that got to him. That there was so much more to *her* than met the eye. That beneath the brilliant, beautiful packaging lay the real Jensen Davis. And as insane as it was, he wanted to see it. He was *intrigued*.

Which was *irrational*, given she was the exact opposite of the type of woman he normally gravitated to—the self-possessed, stable, dependable females he had always chosen—because that's what his life had required. A woman like Alessandra Grasso, a predictable, *safe* choice, with the breeding and power to unite two family dynasties and create an even stronger whole. Something that would only underscore his revival of FV.

The fact that he'd been unable to pull the trigger on that particular match, that he'd told himself it was better done after he'd right-sided FV, when he had the time to invest in a relationship, that he'd harbored niggling doubts about the match, that she wasn't *the one* for him, that had held him back, was beside the point. Jensen Davis was a wild card better left alone.

She swallowed hard. Dragged her gaze from his, as if the exact same thoughts were going through her own head, and glanced at her watch. Finished the last sip of her coffee and set the cup back down in its saucer. "I have to be up at five," she murmured. "I should get some sleep."

"Bene." He shut down his own thoughts that were sure to get him into trouble. "I will walk you back."

Jensen walked with Cristiano back to the pool house, his large palm at the small of her back to guide her across the uneven stones burning a heated imprint into her skin. What on earth was she doing opening up to him like that? Telling him those things about herself? She'd been so intent on steering him away from the truth about Monaco, about her recent headlines, she'd revealed things about herself she'd never told anyone else. How much her career meant to her. The very real fear she had about losing it.

Everything good she'd ever had in her life had disappeared. Her family, when her father had left. The normal life she'd never known she'd craved until she'd been thrust into the spotlight and lost it for good. Any semblance of a maternal instinct her mother might have possessed with the bitter divorce and her one-track focus on the show. She'd always been afraid that would happen to her modeling career, too. That it would vaporize like everything else good in her life. Fears that had been heightened by the missteps of the past few weeks.

She'd seen what it had done to her mother, to lose her movie career. When the beauty you'd traded on faded and you were ruthlessly cast aside for the next bright star. One minute her mother had been a glittering beacon of light, the ultimate Hollywood icon, the next bemused and lost. It was why she'd signed up to do *Hollywood Divas*—because Jensen's father had left her with nothing and she'd needed to survive.

Jensen had sworn it would never happen to her. That she'd build a career so successful, so indestructible, it could never be shattered. Except now, with her mother's ruinous addictions and financial issues, her bank account was empty and that security she'd been building was gone. It made her feel off-balance and scared, something she was afraid Cristiano had picked up on. When exposing vulnerability was the last thing she'd wanted to do. The last thing she *ever* did.

And then there was the part of her that was frightened of what her mother might do, when she'd just assured Cristiano he had nothing to worry about. That her mother's promises only lasted as long as her need for the next big hit. Which wouldn't take long, given how precariously close the show had come to being canceled and the pressure the producers had put her under. She had no idea what her mother would do. A very real fear that made her stomach churn.

She took a deep breath as they reached the pool house, now cast in darkness.

"Oh," she murmured, "I forgot to turn on a light."

She'd never liked darkness. Not since she'd been a child and she and her sisters had been left on their own in bed, while her parents had fought like gladiators, rattling the roof of their Beverly Hills home and raising goose bumps on her skin.

Cristiano released the hand he held to her

back and walked inside, flicking on a lamp in the living room. Jensen followed him inside, where the salon was bathed in a soft, golden glow, her gaze drawn to the hard muscles that flexed and rippled in his back. The amazing arms which she was sure could hold a woman in any position he chose, for as long as he desired. The thought made her throat dry in the dim, intimate confines of the room, mixing with the cavalcade of emotions coursing through her.

He turned around, his azure gaze focusing on her face. On the tumult that raged beneath. He stepped closer, lifted a hand to trace the line of her jaw, sending the most delicate of shivers down her spine. "Jensen," he murmured, "are you okay?"

It might have been the wine, or maybe it was the dark spell that wove itself between them, but she suddenly had the insane urge to tell him everything. To unburden herself of the insanity of the past few months. To explain to Cristiano why her professionalism had suffered of late. But she'd learned from experience that trusting anyone with that kind of knowledge was dangerous, even Cristiano, whom she felt instinctively she could trust. Especially with the secrets her family guarded like the crown jewels. Because they would explode, her mother's secrets, if they ever came to light. It would ruin everything. Not a risk she was prepared to take, no matter how much she wanted to.

"I'm fine," she said huskily. "Just tired."

His blue gaze narrowed. Darkened. She should have thanked him and bid him good-night. Instead, she seemed to gravitate toward him, toward that rock-solid presence he exuded, because even if she couldn't tell him what was eating away at her insides, she could soak up that silent assurance of his. That chemistry that fizzled between them.

His gaze dropped to her mouth, the heat between them banking up into an undeniable force. An instinctual thing, a primal draw that happened every time they came within five feet of each other. A living force that begged to be fulfilled. The wine, which had injected her blood with a heated, sinuous warmth, stripped away her inhibitions, and experiencing what that hard, sensual mouth would feel like on hers became her sole focus. Because she knew it would be amazing. *Life-altering.* And the reckless part of her, the one that always seemed to hold the greatest sway, wanted it. Was only a second away from acting on it.

She heard him mutter a rough oath under his breath, low and thready. It knocked her out of her stupor as effectively as the frigid water she splashed on her face every morning to wake herself up for a shoot.

What was she doing? She knew better than this. They'd just established some sort of rapport between them. Was she really going to mess it up by doing this?

She wasn't sure where her brain had gone, but she needed to find it in a hurry. Because confiding in Cristiano, allowing herself to get involved with him, was stupidity of the highest order when he held her destiny in his hands. When she needed this job more than she'd ever needed one in her life. When opening up to someone else had never been an option for her.

She stepped back. Away from all that hard, muscular warmth. Away from temptation.

"I should get some sleep. *Buona notte,* Cristiano."

CHAPTER FOUR

JENSEN SAT IN the sun-soaked kitchen of the main house, devouring one of Filomena's *cornetto alla crema* along with a cappuccino the house-keeper had made, which were always beyond compare. She'd been working since dawn, her only sustenance an apple for breakfast. Famished, her legs needing a rest, she'd sunk down on one of the kitchen stools when her break had arrived, which, according to most people's schedules, was when they would be leaving for work.

Filomena, busy with her morning duties, had been keeping her company while she baked more *cornetti* and complained about Pedro, the gardener, who had once again overwatered the roses in the garden, which, according to the formidable Italian, looked *tristi e appassiti*, which Jensen had translated loosely with her newly acquired language skills as sad and droopy. She didn't dare disagree with Filomena, because the roses did indeed look unhappy, and furthermore, no one ever disagreed with the housekeeper if they knew what was good for them. Filomena ruled with an iron fist and was proud of it.

Jensen loved these sun-soaked breaks in the kitchen she'd taken to enjoying every morning. Once you got past her outer walls and earned her trust, Filomena was warm and motherly when it came to her charges, which she now considered Jensen to be. Aware of Pascal's complaints his dresses didn't fit, she'd put a fresh tray of pastries in front of Jensen when she'd sat down and ordered her to eat. Which might soon put her in a sugar coma, but it would be well worth it. They were the best thing she'd ever tasted.

It was so nice to have someone take care of her for a change, rather than the other way around—so much of her time spent tracking her mother down and making sure she was on the straight and narrow. A relief to simply sit there and enjoy the sunshine for a few moments while Filomena fussed over her. While the eye of the storm seemed to have passed for the moment.

Alexandre was off in the Caribbean on a whirlwind trip with Juliana working things out, the paparazzi following to capture the drama. The shoot for the collection was going well—

one of her favorites ever. The only thing burrowing away at the back of her mind was the conversation she'd had last night with Scarlett.

Her mother, on a high from her record-level ratings, had been blowing off her appointments with her therapist, insisting she had *everything under control*. Which, to Jensen and her sisters, only meant that her mother was going through another of her manic phases. It was making them all nervous. But given she was thousands of miles away and out of reach, this time it was her sisters Ava and Scarlett's responsibility. A fact she was grateful for, given tonight was the Associazione Nazionale della Moda Italiana party, at which she was to host Ming Li Zhang, a night that had to go seamlessly, without incident.

Filomena regaled her with another colorful tale about the gardener, this time about his encounter with a harmless garden snake, which he had mistaken for a *vipera*. His headlong flight into the kitchen, where he'd snatched up the phone and called the state police, who funneled any kind of emergency to the correct authorities. Only to have the animal expert who'd showed up inform him that the gray-green creature he'd spotted was a garden-variety reptile, whose most harmful property was the foul-smelling odor it emitted when frightened.

"Idiota," Filomena snorted. "Surely he should know."

Jensen bit back laughter. "Perhaps he's had some kind of trauma with snakes."

"Trauma to the head," Filomena suggested, tapping her gray-haired temple.

Jensen burst out laughing. She had just recovered and taken a big bite of the melt-in-your-mouth pastry, when a deep male voice broke up the party.

"Sono in ritardo, Filomena. Un caffè da asporto, per favore."

Cristiano swept into the kitchen, a blur of purposeful motion as he informed the housekeeper he was late and needed his coffee to go. His gaze moved from Filomena to Jensen, who sat frozen, her mouth full of *cornetto*, his eyes a sharp, brilliant blue that rivaled the morning sky. "Care to share the joke?"

She shook her head. Attempted to swallow. He looked *incredible*. Like sex poured into a suit, his long, lithe limbs filled out with enough muscle she decided it must be the perfect ratio. That the suit was clearly custom cut to mold every centimeter of his spectacular body didn't hurt. Clearly one of Pascal's, she concluded, reaching for her cappuccino before she choked on the pastry she'd consumed.

Disaster averted, she set the cup down. "You're late leaving today."

"An early conference call. I did it from here." He leaned a hip against the counter as Filomena bustled around, preparing his espresso. Moved his gaze down over the sweep of her cheek, to her full mouth, resting there in a lingering appraisal that made her cheeks heat. "You have chocolate on your face."

She lifted a hand. Scrubbed self-consciously at her mouth. "I was starving. They're so good, I couldn't stop."

His mouth curved in an amused smile. "The breakfast of champions, clearly."

Jensen's stomach flip-flopped. She could ignore the attraction between them when he was being his typical arrogant, slightly insufferable self. It was a whole other ball game when he turned on the charm. Given she'd spent the last few days studiously avoiding him after that *almost-kiss* the other night, in which she'd nearly done something stupid and unwise, as she suspected he himself had been doing, it felt like a minor setback. However, she concluded, inhaling a deep breath, sanity had now prevailed, and she was intent on sticking with it.

"All good?" he probed, his azure gaze speculative, sensing her inner turbulence.

"Perfetto," she replied, plastering a smooth, even-keeled look across her face.

"Bene." He surveyed her a moment longer before accepting the coffee Filomena handed him with a murmured thanks. "I thought," he drawled, "that we could attend the party together tonight. We are meeting the Zhangs at the event. You can occupy Ming Li, show her a good time, while I work through some things with Nicholas."

Spend the entire evening with him? Her heartbeat quickened at the idea, accompanied by an equally strong surge of dismay. Surely that wasn't necessary? But, she conceded, if the plan was for her to show Ming Li a good time while Cristiano schmoozed Nicholas Zhang, she would hardly spend much time at his side. Very little, in fact. *Safe*, in the great scheme of things.

"Fine," she agreed. "Will we leave from here?"

"Si. I will pick you up when I get home from the office."

She nodded. He pushed away from the counter and picked up his briefcase. She was halfway out of her chair, plate in hand, when he stopped in the doorway, his broad shoulders filling the frame.

"Jensen?"

She looked up at him.

"Ming Li is an impressionable sixteen-year-old. Keep it PG tonight."

She absorbed the concern written across his face. He really had bought into the headlines about her. Which, until the past few weeks, had been an ancient replica of her that had nothing to do with reality. It dug into her gut, stoked the frustration simmering inside her. Because that wasn't her anymore. But all she could do was swallow it and let him think what he was destined to do.

"I will be on my best behavior," she assured him, hiking her chin. "Strike any worries from your head."

The paparazzi were lined up three rows deep at La Scala as the world's glitterati arrived to celebrate the current innovators of Italian fashion. The cocktail reception, held in the Palazzo La Scala outside the majestic opera house, was in full swing as Jensen and Cristiano stepped from his midnight-blue two-seater on a still-warm, sultry night, black-coated waitstaff serving cocktails in advance of the dinner to follow, a string quartet providing the music.

All eyes were on them as they worked the red carpet, done tonight in Italy's national colors of red, green and white, negotiating the blindingly powerful camera flashes as they stopped to greet the people they knew, the crowd a virtual who's who of global fashion.

They made their way toward the step-and-repeat banner emblazoned with the logos of the famous Italian fashion conglomerates represented that evening. Besieged with questions about Prince Alexandre and the current scandal, Jensen refused to give credence to the tabloid rumors tossed at them from the teeming pack of hungry reporters, focusing instead on presenting the details of Francesco's dress she was wearing.

Together, she and Cristiano worked their way through the crowd. If she could sense the gossip percolating beneath the surface of the aristocratic gathering, with herself and the prince as its focus, perfectly concealed in that cultured, subtle way the Milanese used to dig their way beneath your skin, it was blunted by Cristiano's presence at her side. An absolute refusal by the elite to visibly slight a gilded member of that aristocracy, despite the chatter happening beneath the surface.

A glass of champagne in her hand, Cristiano's palm at her back, she focused on dazzling the crowd. Exchanging the witty repartee she was known for. And if his touch evoked a warm, tingling sensation, a reaction she couldn't seem to avoid, as the man himself did, she ignored it. Because tonight, she was not going to get sidetracked. *Distracted.* Ambushed. Tonight she was going to be *perfect*. Her career depended on it.

Midway through the packed throng, she felt Cristiano's attention shift, his fingers tightening at her back, before he bent his head to hers. "Nicholas Zhang and his daughter are on your right. In the black tux and the fire-engine-red dress."

Jensen took in the distinguished-looking Zhang, known for his cutthroat deal-making. Handsome in the stern, aristocratic sense, with an aquiline nose, the sharp, hard lines of his face seemed to reflect his legendary personality. His daughter, on the other hand, was delicate and lovely, with luminous dark eyes and a perfect oval face, framed by a swath of silky dark hair. She also, clearly, had a formidable fashion sense in the way she wore the gorgeous red silk dress Jensen and the design team had sent over, with a scarf and glittering heels to match.

Cristiano made the introductions. Nicholas Zhang clasped her hand in a firm grip, his sharp gaze assessing. Then he introduced his daughter, Ming Li, who proffered a delicate hand to Jensen, an animated expression on her beautiful face.

"Thank you so much for the dress. It's perfect."

"Thank Pascal," Jensen deferred to the brilliant designer. "You look gorgeous in it."

"*You* are even more beautiful in person. I begged my father to bring me with him, because I wanted to meet you."

"That's very sweet of you to say." She acknowledged the compliment with a smile. "You are quite stunning yourself."

"I want to be a model," said Nicholas's daughter, her chin lifting, "but my father is dead set against it. He wants me to go to business school so I can run the company someday."

"Which you will," her father inserted evenly.

Jensen stifled a smile at the exchange. "It isn't all glamour, you know…modeling. It's a lot of hard work. Long days."

Ming Li rolled her eyes. "So is keeping my four-point-zero GPA."

Jensen noted the very American term. "You go to school in the US?"

Nicholas's daughter nodded. "Father wanted me to have an international view to the world. I go to boarding school in Connecticut."

Jensen wasn't inclined to disagree with her father. Modeling was a viciously competitive world. Few models ever made it to the top. And even when they did, that success could be fleeting. It had always been her biggest regret having begun modeling at sixteen, that she had just a GED designation to her credit through her private tutors, her schedule making it too difficult for her to attend school. Something she'd always felt she'd missed out on.

But she also wasn't in the business of raining on other people's dreams, because she knew what her own had meant to her. How reaching for the seemingly unattainable could push a person past what they thought they were capable of. She flicked her gaze to the two men, intent on giving Cristiano the time with Nicholas Zhang he'd desired. "Perhaps I can introduce Ming Li around? There are scads of famous designers and models here tonight. Some real legends."

Ming Li's eyes lit up. "That would be amazing."

Her father eyed her with a firm look. "If you behave yourself."

"Of course." Ming Li hooked an arm through Jensen's. "Introduce me to *everyone*. Don't leave anyone out. I want to meet them all."

Cristiano shot her an amused look, his gaze seeming to convey a mixture of gratitude and wariness. She sent him a reassuring look back, ordering her heart not to beat in triple time at how insanely handsome he was in the dark tux. Then she and Ming Li disappeared into the crowd.

"God," the teenager said, exhaling on a sigh, "It is so *stifling* being with him. I need a break." She scooped a glass of champagne off a waiter's tray and laced her arm through Jensen's. "Cristiano, on the other hand, is amazing. I know he's too old for me," she said at the look Jensen threw her. "I'm not totally deluded. However," she added on an airy breath, "I want the full scoop on everything. The prince. The affair. The truth behind all the rumors."

Jensen plucked the glass from her hand and returned it to a passing waiter's tray. "That will not endear me to your father. Secondly," she added, procuring a frothy nonalcoholic cocktail for the teenager, "I hate to burst your bubble, but there is no affair with the prince. I can, however, introduce you to David Swanson. He's here somewhere. Will that do?"

A dazed look crossed the teenager's face at the mention of one of Hollywood's leading men. "You aren't serious."

"Very. He's a personal friend of mine. In fact, I see him now. Let's go say hello."

Cristiano watched as Jensen worked the crowd, Ming Li at her side, the brightest light in a sea of glittering stars. Clad in an ethereal creation of Francesco's, its blush-nude hue the perfect contrast for her dark eyes and olive skin, the bespoke organic silk georgette gown had a flowing, fairy-tale-like silhouette. But the gown was not all innocence with its plunging neckline that skimmed the curves of her breasts, its clever cutouts that revealed tantalizing glimpses of smooth, creamy skin, and elegant crisscrossing straps that left her back bare to the waist.

She was shockingly beautiful. There wasn't a man in the crowd who hadn't had his eyes on her at one point or another. It was, however, the light that seemed to emanate from her that captured him. How everyone she talked to seemed drawn to her in that inevitable way that he was. There wasn't a sign of the vulnerable, complex creature he'd witnessed at dinner the other night. Instead, it was all the glittering glory of Jensen Davis, supremely in her element. And while he appreciated the perfect show as the representative of his brand, what he himself had asked for, he found himself wondering what was going on in her head as she flitted from group to group, as elusive as the most vibrant butterfly.

What made her tick. Why she refused to let anyone get too close. Why she spread those delicate wings of hers and took flight when anyone did. If the truth be known, he hadn't been able to get her out of his head all week after that almost-kiss, which had seemed to occupy far too many of his thoughts. They had a physical chemistry that couldn't be denied, that was clear. But it was more, this curiosity of his he couldn't seem to escape.

She had been tireless in her work ethic since she'd arrived, completing every one of her responsibilities with that vivacious energy she possessed, including a charitable event with young, at-risk girls in which, according to his staff, she'd shone, her natural warmth and empathy on full magnetic display. Perhaps, he pondered, it had been her own chaotic upbringing that had contributed to that sense of connection between her and the other women.

"She is a shining star," Nicholas Zhang murmured, following Cristiano's gaze across the crowd to where Jensen stood. "A masterful play on your part, Vitale. Brands can no longer afford to simply sit on the sidelines and ignore the fact that influence is fast moving to the social space. To marry that strategy with such a legendary brand, to take that risk, was pure genius."

Cristiano had long ago decided the risk was worth the reward. That big gambles were the only way he was going to save his legacy. A play he hoped wouldn't blow up in his face, given the complex, multifaceted plan he'd crafted, the gamble he'd taken on the man standing in front of him the key to it all. It wasn't a vision he could second-guess now, at its most critical juncture.

"I think," he said deliberately, transferring his gaze from Jensen to the cutthroat billionaire, "it's time we take the gloves off and discuss the real issues at hand, don't you? Get this deal done."

Nicholas Zhang's dark gaze gleamed at the challenge. "I never did like doing business with a suite of lawyers in the room. Throw in a '46 Macallan and we can get down to it."

Jensen returned Ming Li to her father after dinner, which gave Cristiano a good deal of time to work through his issues with Nicholas Zhang. She felt lighter than she had in weeks. Buoyed by her success as she and Cristiano waved the Zhangs off. Not only had she shown Ming Li a good time, chock-full of all the biggest celebrities, she'd also had the brilliant idea to take the younger woman backstage at Pascal's debut show. A once-in-a-lifetime opportunity she hoped would help cement Cristiano's deal.

Cristiano frowned as she recounted the offer. "Are you sure you want to take that on? There will be a lot going on that night."

She brushed the objection aside. "It will be

brilliant for her. There is no experience like it. Nicholas will be there, the excitement will translate to him and it will be a moment she'll never forget. Plus, if Ming Li is serious about a career in modeling, she will also get to see the pressure, the intensity of it all. If she still wants to do it after that, she will have the full picture. She will *know*."

A reluctant smile curved his mouth. "In that case, I think it's a fantastic idea. I'm hoping to have the deal done by then, but if anything, it will provide a very resounding exclamation point to the night. *Grazie mille*," he murmured, fixing those amazing blue eyes on her, "for everything you've done tonight. Ming Li clearly had a wonderful time."

She tried to ignore how that meltingly slow smile affected her insides. Lit a flush beneath her skin that seemed to spread body-wide. "It was nothing. I had fun. Did you get things ironed out with Nicholas?"

A frown creased his brow. "There are a few things left to finesse. Speaking of which," he said, nodding toward his family, congregated at the bar, "I should give them an update."

She balked when he set a hand to her waist and would have propelled her there, the idea of facing Cristiano's supremely aristocratic family with the rumors about her and Alexandre still circulating distinctly unappealing. Federico, Cristiano's uncle, had always been somewhat aloof; Marcella, his grandmother, the matriarch of the family, was frankly terrifying; Ilaria, Cristiano's sister, who headed up FV's public relations, the only Vitale she had a warm relationship with.

"I have a few people I should say hello to," she protested. "Perhaps I should—"

"Afterward," he interrupted, brushing over her protest and shepherding her toward his family. "This won't take long. Ilaria made me promise to bring you by. She saw the proofs of the collection and is over the moon."

Jensen acquiesced, if reluctantly. She did love Ilaria, and she was equally excited about the shoot. Squaring her shoulders, she allowed Cristiano to guide her to where his family stood assembled at the bar, set up outside on the warm, sultry night. She greeted Federico, Cristiano's uncle and head of the company's Italian operations, first, who offered a cool if polite greeting, then Marcella. If the ice-cold look on the silver-haired matriarch's elegantly lined face was anything to go by, she'd been right in her presumptions. Marcella had heard the gossip about Alexandre and was less than impressed.

She exchanged perfunctory kisses with the matriarch, steeling herself against the icy chill directed her way, then turned and greeted Ilaria, brushing a kiss to the tall, attractive brunette's cheek.

"Don't mind her," Ilaria murmured, pressing a kiss to her other cheek. "She just received an earful from the church about your dip in the fountain. They are all quite scandalized. She is also a personal friend of Queen Sofia, so you're hitting her from all angles. You look amazing, by the way."

Jensen cast a thankful look at Ilaria as she pressed a glass of champagne into her hands. She'd been intent on nursing one glass the entire night in an attempt to keep her head clear, but for *this*, she just might need it.

Ilaria drew her into conversation while Cristiano and Federico talked business. Ilaria's illustrious MBA and whip-smart brain had earned her the director of communications job at FV at age thirty, an impressive feat by anyone's standards. Yet she had always picked Jensen's brain on marketing, recognizing her social influence and her ability to reach the young women who were crucial to the brand.

She and Ilaria talked strategy until Cristiano and Federico concluded their rather heated discussion and joined in, the conversation shifting to the busy fall fashion season ahead and FV's fiftieth anniversary party, which would kick off

Milan Fashion Week, highlighting Francesco's historic contributions to Italian fashion. The perfect precursor to Pascal's spectacular debut collection for FV, which would follow at the end of the week.

The anniversary party, which Ilaria was organizing, would be a star-studded event, hosted at a glorious Milanese landmark. Jensen found herself entranced by Ilaria's brilliant idea of ending the evening with an auction of Francesco's most famous dresses, one from every year he'd been designing, with the proceeds donated to the local hospital charity Marcella sat on the board of.

"It will be magical," Jensen murmured, her brain conjuring up all sorts of wonderful images.

"*Si.*" Ilaria sighed. "I love the idea. But I'm afraid I've bitten off more than I can chew. My team is maxed, and it's a logistical beast curating all the gowns."

Jensen was still caught up in the magic of it all. "How are you going to display them?"

"A museum-like retrospective…we have a beautiful open space to do it in."

A vision built itself in Jensen's head, layer building upon layer. "What if you did it live instead? Used some of the original models who wore the dresses… I'm sure there will be quite a few of them attending the party."

A glitter entered Ilaria's eyes. "Oh," she breathed, "that would be incredible. What a story it would be. The original supermodels in the original dresses. It would blow the roof off the night."

"You have no time," Cristiano interjected. "You are already working until midnight every evening."

Whereas she had time, Jensen thought, chewing on her lip. The collection was almost shot, the television commercial the last big piece to come. "I could do it," she offered. "I have the contacts. I could pull in some favors from friends to fill out the lineup. Handle the logistics of the auction for you so it would free up your time. I've done a million charity events like this."

"I don't think that's a good idea." Marcella interjected, directing a pointed look at Jensen. "This is not a publicity stunt to flog the Vitale name. The type of…sensational, headline-grabbing events you are used to. It is a serious charitable endeavor that requires class and commitment. It's the biggest event this company has done in its history. It needs to be done right."

Jensen's fingers tightened around her glass, the insinuation she had no class stinging her skin. She was used to the criticism of her scandalous family and the manufactured celebrity it traded on. And yes, many of the events she'd done as a Davis had been just such high-profile occasions designed to generate headlines. But they had also been rooted in good—her mother a champion of the community. To have Marcella throw it in her face like that, when she'd spent the past year devoting herself to putting FV back on the map again, was just too much to take.

Cristiano, who'd detected the temperature change, set a warm palm to her waist, but she ignored it, too annoyed to heed it. Directed a pointed look at Marcella. "I am well aware of the importance of this event," she said evenly. "And I understand the last few weeks have been a bit rocky—something that I apologize for. I will do better. But if the purpose of this auction is to draw attention to an historic anniversary for the brand as well as generate profile for a good cause, *that* is something I know how to do. I am well aware of what the *tone* should be."

Ilaria flicked a glance from her grandmother to Jensen, clearly attempting to figure out how to navigate this battle. "The photo of Jensen at the AMAs is the most popular post on Instagram this year," she pointed out. "*Fifteen million* people have liked it. The PR department has been deluged with inquiries on where to buy Pascal's dress. I think she could really help us move the needle on this."

Marcella opened her mouth to object, but Cristiano silenced her with a wave of his hand. "I think it's an excellent idea," he weighed in. "The PR department will appreciate another charitable activity on Jensen's part, given the recent headlines. Jensen clearly has the clout to help Ilaria blow this thing out of the water. It makes perfect sense. Of course," he concluded, "she will be wearing the final dress of the evening as the current face of the brand."

Marcella raised a silver brow, as if to ask her grandson if he knew the disaster he was inviting. Cristiano ignored it completely. "It's decided, then. I think it's a fantastic idea."

Jensen was still fuming when Cristiano separated them from his family and shepherded her through the crowd, the party still going strong as guests enjoyed after-dinner drinks and dancing in the square, champagne flowing from fountains like water, the elegant fairy-tale lighting in the palazzo casting a warm glow over the night. Deciding she needed a few moments to cool down, and done with his quota of small talk for the evening, Cristiano directed her toward the dance floor, set off by a series of twinkling lights.

"I think," he murmured, "we should dance."

A look he couldn't read moved across her face. "I'm fine," she said quickly. "We're pretty much finished now anyway, aren't we? Always best to end these things on a high note."

"You have smoke coming out of your ears. One dance," he insisted, "and then we will go. Also," he added helpfully, nodding at a point over her shoulder, "Beryl Morgan is on her way over." One of Milan's most outrageous gossip bloggers, she was known for her vicious virtual red pen. "Unless you'd like to give her the un-adulterated scoop."

Jensen's face telegraphed her horror at the prospect. She followed him onto the dance floor then, taking the hand he extended, a slight flush lighting her high cheekbones as he pulled her closer before placing his other hand at the small of her back, his palm absorbing the warmth of her bare, silky skin revealed by the daring dress. It was even softer than he could have imagined. Lacing his fingers through hers, he pulled her a step closer, until the scent of her delicate floral perfume infiltrated his senses.

It was still a very respectable hold. But with that innate chemistry between them crackling to life and sensitizing every one of his nerve endings, they might as well have been cheek to cheek in the way that she affected him. *Vastly. Completely.*

His heartbeat quickened in his chest, his blood sliding through his veins on a heady pull, his every sense attuned to her. He was fairly sure she felt it, too, from the way her breath caught in her throat, the way she seemed to focus everywhere but on him, staring at the lapel of his jacket for long moments, before she finally looked up at him. And then there was no mistaking the heat that smoldered between them, the flames in her dark eyes spilling out and licking across his skin.

"I'm sorry," she said, in what seemed like a valiant effort to deflect from it, "about your grandmother. I just get so frustrated when people have these preconceived notions about me."

"Preconceived?" He arched a dark brow at her. "You do stoke the flames, you have to admit. Give her some time," he advised. "Do the job I know you can do with the anniversary party. She will come around."

She didn't look entirely convinced, a battle going on in those luminous ebony eyes of hers. He sought to explain, to calm the turbulence emanating from her. "All she sees are the publicity stunts your family engages in. The headlines surrounding the events your mother puts on, which Marcella then interprets as a less-than-altruistic cause."

"Which might be absolutely true," she agreed, her beautiful face expressive. "She does do sensational things for the media coverage. For the *buzz*. But there is also good in what she does. She has always been a keen supporter of the community. Those causes she supports *mean* something to her. She puts an incredible amount of work into them. As much as Marcella does. Yet look at how she is treated."

Loyalty, he registered. Another facet of her he was discovering. That same loyalty she'd displayed toward his brand, that he hadn't been fully aware of. Her refusal, even now, to criticize her mother, who according to those who knew Veronica Davis was a master strategist, moving her daughters around like chess pieces.

"No doubt," he conceded softly, "she does good work. My grandmother was harsh. She can be that way. She only sees one right way of doing things, and that is based in propriety—what she's been schooled in. It was not, however, fair of her to pass judgment on your family in that way. I apologize for her behavior."

She was silent, whatever was going on behind those darks eyes still festering. He tightened his fingers around hers. *"Che cosa?"* he murmured. *What?* "Talk to me."

"That's the way I used to be," she admitted. "I used to 'stoke the flames.' Be as outrageous as I could possibly be, because that worked for me. It got me the attention I was looking for. It got me star status on the show. But I am not that person anymore." Her mouth twisted on a frustrated curve. "I made the decision to walk away from the show. To be someone different. But it always seems to come back to haunt me."

"Because you are your own worst enemy," he opined. "All my grandmother sees, all the *world* sees, is a vision of you, without your clothes, frolicking in that fountain. Being outrageous for the sake of being outrageous. And," he proposed, "where has it gotten you?"

A myriad of emotions flickered across her face. He thought for a moment she might answer, then he watched her retreat. Slide a veil over those dark eyes, and it irritated him. Perhaps because he'd seen more of her now. Enough to know she was hiding behind this public persona of herself she'd manufactured that he didn't think had anything to do with reality. "Why," he pushed softly, his eyes on hers, "do you do these self-destructive things to yourself?"

She sank her teeth into the plump skin of her lush lower lip. Eyed him. "I don't know," she said finally. "Maybe I get drawn back in sometimes, when I shouldn't. Maybe I make bad de-

cisions in the moment, based on my history."
She hiked a shoulder. "Maybe it's easier to be
that version of myself, because that's what people expect of me. Which I always regret after
the fact."

He absorbed the vulnerable curve of her
mouth. The deep internal conflict written across
her face. He didn't understand it, because he'd
never operated that way himself. He'd always
learned from his mistakes and moved on as a
more self-aware version of himself. But with
Jensen, it was more complex. If a half real, half
manufactured world was all she'd ever known,
sliding back into it would be far too easy, given
the right incentive. Of which there were many.

"You must recognize the folly in that," he
murmured. "It will never end. You will keep
getting drawn in. It's the nature of that world."

"I know." Her mouth turned down. "It was a
moment of weakness. I went against my better
judgment, only to have it blow up in my face."

"So you learn from your mistake. Make better decisions next time. You know who you are,
Jensen. Who you want to be. You made that decision when you walked away from the show."

She nodded. "I know. You're right."

And that, he concluded from the shuttered
look on her face, was all he was going to get.
Which was more than what he'd been able to

glean from her thus far. It should have been a red flag for him that she was far from a sure bet. That she had a tendency to fall back into old habits. That he should keep his guard up. Instead, it was her vulnerability that got to him. The bizarre urge he felt to protect her from this crazy world she'd been born into. All mixed up with an attraction he couldn't seem to ignore. The way she moved him in a way he couldn't seem to understand.

His hand dropped lower on her hip, the delicate scent of her perfume filling his head. He felt, *heard*, the quickening of her breath as his hold shifted that much closer and his breath skated across her temple. The heat of his palm sinking into the curve of her hip, her soft contours melted into him, fitting perfectly against the hard planes of his body, as if she was made for him. And then, it was only them, the noise of the buzzing crowd receding as the force of their attraction ignited.

It was becoming an almost compulsive urge to know her, to explore the chemistry between them. To harness all of that vibrancy for himself, to hell with his better instincts. Because he knew it would be like nothing else he'd ever felt. That it would light him up in a way he'd never experienced before. As irrational as it was, as unadvisable as it was, it was also undeniable.

The moment hung there, thick and uncharted, neither of them daring to break it, because it was just that powerful. Until the last notes of the music played and the spell was broken. Aware of where they were, of the eyes on them, he stepped back, reluctantly releasing Jensen from his hold.

"It's getting late," he said huskily, his gaze on hers. "You have to get up early for work. Let's say good-night to the organizers and I'll get the car."

Jensen waited near the exit for Cristiano to collect the car, her head reeling from that moment between them on the dance floor. It had felt *real*, tangible, the connection between them. Unmistakable this time. She could have sworn that had been regret in his eyes when he'd released her. That he'd been as loath to break the moment as she had. It had her insides in a tangle, her heart beating far too fast. Because if it was *real*, if there was something between them, what was she going to do about it?

Ignore it. She had promised herself she wasn't going to do this. That she was going to focus on the job at hand and nothing more. And then Marcella had torn a strip off of her and it had all gone sideways. She'd been so stung by the Vitale matriarch's treatment of her, had felt so *humiliated*, so unfairly judged, she'd felt compelled to defend herself to Cristiano.

She'd thrown pieces of the old Jensen at him to justify her behavior. She wasn't sure he'd completely bought it, but it had been the best she could do to steer him away from the truth about her mother. As for the intense connection they shared that seemed to build with every encounter? She blamed it on her vulnerability in the moment. Her uncertainty of what her mother would do in this manic state of hers. Maybe she'd wanted to lean on Cristiano in the midst of the storm. Take refuge. But it was his reaction to their conversation that had thrown her.

Unlike her ex, Daniel, who had walked away from her when her reality show life had proven too much, Cristiano hadn't seemed to judge her for it. Instead, he'd seemed to understand, to *empathize* even. It had her feeling distinctly off-balance and uncertain, because experience had taught her that her past would always be used against her, that *she* would always be judged by it. She'd taught herself it would be naive to think it would ever be any different. To protect herself against future hurt. And yet Cristiano *had* reacted differently.

Her heart beating far too loud in her chest, her legs a little unsteady, she sat down on a low concrete wall while she waited. When several minutes had passed and it seemed to be taking Cristiano a long time to return with the car, she got up and went looking for him, too tired and exhausted to sit still. Found him standing near the valet stand, talking to a tall, leggy blonde.

The woman's honey-colored hair cut into a chic bob that skimmed her shoulders, she had delicate, finely boned features, big blue eyes and effortless style in the sapphire-blue sheath dress she wore. An air of confidence that came from her roots in one of Milan's oldest, most aristocratic families made Alessandra Grasso the perfect choice for Cristiano, according to the models who'd pointed her out earlier. Everything she was not.

It had been the subject of a full-fledged gossip discussion, Ming Li looking on with avid curiosity while the models had engaged in innuendo-fueled speculation. Whether or not Cristiano would finally pull the trigger and marry Alessandra. How, even if they'd had their rocky times, she was still destined for him—the heir to an Italian textile dynasty, who could unite two Italian fashion legends. And Alessandra, according to the models, tended to get what she was after.

Jensen felt as if she'd been socked in the chest as she watched them talk, Cristiano's dark, handsome head bent to Alessandra's, the intimacy of the moment clear. She really had to get over this infatuation she had with him. The belief that there was something between them, when in actual fact, she was the last female he'd ever get involved with, even if there was a blatant attraction between them. Because he would end up with a woman like Alessandra Grasso, not someone like her. It was preordained.

His family had made it clear what they thought of her tonight. That she was the kind of scandalous American reality show trash she was so often billed as. To think Cristiano would think differently, despite his outward empathy, was naive. Which meant she needed to get her head together and fast.

When Cristiano finally returned, car keys dangling from his fingers, her composure was restored. "Are you all right?" He eyed her with a look of concern.

"Perfect," she murmured. "Just tired. Are we ready?"

He gave her a long look, then nodded and held the car door open so she could get in. Then he got behind the wheel of the low-slung sports car. They made the drive home in silence, a palpable tension throbbing between them she made no attempt to address. When they stopped in the circular driveway of the villa, and Cristiano got out to walk around to her side of the car and open the door for her, she slid out and took a step backward, away from his tall, overpowering presence. *"Buona notte,"* she murmured. "Thank you for a lovely night."

Jensen couldn't sleep. Her head was too full, her thoughts too disordered since she'd walked away from Cristiano earlier. Which should have been the right decision. Which *was* the right decision. But she couldn't stop thinking about it. About that moment between them on the dance floor. Couldn't get it out of her head.

She was also hungry. *Starving.* She'd done so much socializing, intent on showing Ming Li a good time, she'd barely eaten anything. Her stomach rumbled, a headache threatened, and a vision of Filomena's delicious homemade bread filled her head, topped with a thick slice of Italian cheese. And once there, she couldn't get rid of it.

She was never going to sleep. And, given she needed a good rest before tomorrow's shoot, waking up with a stormy head wouldn't be an auspicious start. Gathering her hair into a ponytail and pulling on delicate, bejeweled flip-flops, she slipped out the door and headed toward the main house, the interior of the villa cast in darkness in the late hour.

Filomena was off tonight, but she'd told Jensen to help herself if she ever needed anything. Slipping into the warm, inviting kitchen, where a lamp was always left on in case someone needed something, she poured herself a glass of milk and made a sandwich with the thick, delicious bread. Seated on the marble countertop, she absorbed the peace of the night, an army of cicadas singing their song through the big, open bay windows, moonlight flooding the fragrant gardens outside.

She had just finished her sandwich and was reaching for her glass of milk when Cristiano walked into the kitchen, another pair of those dark, sexy denims slung low over his lean hips, a black T-shirt hugging his muscular torso. Distracted and disheveled, as if he'd pushed his hand through his hair a dozen times, he looked up to see her perched on the counter, the glass of milk poised halfway to her mouth.

She wasn't sure what rendered her off-balance more—how insanely good he looked in the casual clothes, clinging to all of that honed, delicious muscle, or the fact that she was perched on his kitchen counter in a camisole and short pajamas that had seemed perfectly appropriate in the intimate confines of her cottage, but now with his dark perusal raking over her, absorbing every detail, felt far too revealing.

He moved his gaze down, over the long, bare

length of her legs, up over the smooth skin of her thighs, then higher, to where the camisole clung to her curves. This time, when he lifted his gaze up to hers, he didn't attempt to hide the dark embers that glimmered there. To deny this crazy attraction between them. Instead, he moved closer, coming to a halt a few inches in front of her.

Jensen set the glass on the counter, her fingers shaking slightly. She could feel the heat that emanated from him, bleeding into her skin. Her bones. She'd never met a man so *male*, in the true sense of the word. So earthily attractive. And she worked with some of the world's most beautiful men.

A flush bloomed in her chest, moving up to consume her cheeks. It felt like she was on fire, but she was fairly certain most of that was the internal combustion they created together.

"I thought," she said haltingly, "that everyone had gone to bed. I haven't eaten much all day. Filomena said to help myself. So I—" she waved a hand at the cupboard "—made a sandwich."

"You were busy with Ming Li. You must be hungry." He thrust his fingers through his hair in an action that only increased his disheveled look. "I had a conference call with Brazil. It ran late."

She absorbed the deep shadows underlining

his eyes. His palpable exhaustion. "You should get some sleep," she murmured, her breath feeling a little trapped in her throat. "You have Zhang in hand. Everything else can wait until the morning, no?"

Cristiano knew he should. Go to bed. He was beyond coherent at this point he was so exhausted. But he couldn't seem to make himself move. Not when she looked like his every fantasy come true in those provocative silk pajamas, which put those long, incredible legs of hers on full, magnificent display. Not when every brain cell he possessed was focused on the voluptuous curve of her breasts the silky material hinted at, making him wonder what she'd feel like in his hands. When beneath the vulnerable curve of her mouth and the wary cast of her eyes lay the same burning fire consuming him.

He tightened his hands into fists at his sides. Unfurled them slowly. Fought it valiantly, because surely this was a bad idea. He'd been telling himself that ever since she'd walked away from him earlier, as if the hounds of hell had been at her heels. Over the past couple of hours, as he'd sought to find a solution to Zhang's aggressive demands that his family and the board could live with, a delicate minefield he had to tread carefully. Which had been the smart thing to do. Was still the smart thing to do.

He exhaled a deep breath. Moved to the water cooler, where he poured himself a tall glass of water, and stood, leaning against the counter as he downed half of it in one go. Inhaled a deep breath to deliver some much-needed oxygen to his brain, which he wasn't sure was going to do much good with the heat smoking through the kitchen. "Zhang threw a few monkey wrenches my way tonight. I've been trying to untangle them."

She cocked a brow. "What kind of monkey wrenches?"

"A larger say in what FV does. Creative input in the brand. A seat on the board, which I had anticipated. The rest not so much."

"Oh." She absorbed the information. "That won't go over well with your family, will it?"

"No. My grandfather was not for giving up any control of FV to outside influences. Neither is Federico. I've convinced him we either make this play, or we dig our own grave as we lapse into irrelevancy. Zhang, however, is driving a hard bargain."

She sank her teeth into her lip, worrying the tender flesh. "Nicholas is undeniably brilliant. He understands the global marketplace and he understands how customers are consuming fashion. Get Ilaria to pull the spring campaign he did for Kyra and show it to Federico. When you dig into it, it's a complete masterpiece. It will demonstrate his worth."

"That's a good idea." He rubbed a palm against his temple. "Maybe I will. Zhang also thinks we should expand our influencer base. Develop some branded lines to target different lifestyle segments. You could be valuable input on this."

She nodded. "Anytime. Just say the word. And I'm sure your family will come around. You haven't made a wrong decision yet." She slid to the edge of the counter, the nervousness of her movement betraying the tension between them. Tension that had been seething between them for days. Tension that had been occupying far too much of his head.

And suddenly, he didn't want to avoid it anymore. He wanted to confront it, because he didn't think it was going anywhere. If anything, it was only getting worse.

"Maybe," he murmured, setting his gaze on hers, "you'd like to tell me why you ran away from me earlier. The car had barely come to a stop and you were hightailing it back to the pool house."

Her ebony eyes widened. Darkened. "I wasn't running away. I was tired."

"And that's why you did the same thing after dinner the other night…because you were tired? Because it seems to me, this attraction between us is clear. What we need to do is decide what to do about it."

"Ignore it," she said instantly. "I work for you, Cristiano. We need to keep a professional relationship."

"You work for yourself," he returned, eyeing the flash of heat that had consumed her creamy cheeks. "The only reason I stepped in in London was because you weren't living up to the terms of your contract. Now that we have that out of the way, I think it's time we faced this thing between us."

"I don't," she said staunchly. "If we were smart, we would shut this down now. Get the sleep we both clearly need."

But neither of them were that smart, clearly, or one of them would have moved. Put an end to the madness. And quite frankly, he was tired of fighting it. Couldn't even, in this moment, as she stared at him with those big brown eyes, her chest moving too quickly up and down, betraying how very affected she was, remember why this wasn't a good idea. Because surely it was not. Because it felt like the most natural thing in the world. Like if he just reached out and touched her, something inside him would be alive again. Which was either his fatigued brain playing tricks on him, or a truth he wasn't willing to admit. And he couldn't, for the life of him, stop himself from taking a step closer.

"I would," he said huskily, "because there is no question I need sleep. That this is, perhaps, not a good idea. But I'm afraid if I did, I would not be able to get this out of my head."

Her eyes widened. Dark, decadent pools of temptation that beckoned him in. "Get what out of your head?"

"This," he breathed, setting both hands on the counter to brace his arms on either side of her. Which only served to send the delicate floral scent of her perfume wafting through his head, intoxicating him on a whole other level. Because it was mixed with *her*—that irresistible, delectable, heady scent that was hers alone.

He stayed there, resisting the urge to move, waiting for a sign from her that she did not want this, because then he could have walked away. *Would* have walked away. Waited for some glimpse of sanity from either of them. Instead, she tipped her head back, her silky hair falling over the bare skin of her shoulder, her dark eyes stormy. He was fairly sure she wasn't breathing, or barely if she was, the pulse at the base of her throat throbbing in a sign he could not have missed.

It was all the invitation he needed. Shifting his weight to one hand, he reached up and set his thumb to the mad beat at the juncture of her neck and throat. Absorbed the frantic pulse that pounded there. It satisfied him in a way he could not begin to describe.

Sliding his fingers up to the curve of her jaw, he held her where he wanted her, bending his head to slide his mouth against the velvety surface of her cheek. Against the delicate curve of her mouth. She sucked in a breath as he took his time, exploring the contours of her mouth, learning every soft facet of her, every centimeter of her lush skin, the mouth of a siren, designed to drive a man wild. When he had prolonged the anticipation, when his name was a barely audible whisper on the air, ripped from her lips, he covered the vulnerable curve of her mouth with his.

Slow, deliberate, *thorough,* he explored every dip and valley of her mouth, satisfying every curiosity he'd ever had about what she felt like. What she tasted like. What it would *be* like to touch her. And if he were being honest, the fantasies he'd indulged in far too frequently of late. When she lifted a delicate hand to tangle her fingers into the hair at the base of his skull and pulled him closer, her breath mingling with his, he deepened the kiss into a more sensual exploration, his fingers curving around her jaw to hold her still.

When she moaned, a low, needy sound that came from deep in her throat, it was an intoxicating admission that electrified him. Pulled him in deeper. Sliding his hands down to her hips, he pulled her closer, her lush, full bottom filling his palms. Which only intoxicated him further, because she was silky soft beneath his hands. Even better than he'd imagined.

Hotter, brighter, the kiss burned, until it was no longer enough to satisfy either of them. His hands guiding her closer to the edge of the counter, he slid his fingers underneath the straps of her camisole, any common sense he might have possessed dissipating on a surge of lust. He dragged the thin straps of the negligible piece of silk down, exposing the full, ripe curves of her breasts. Taut, perfectly shaped and rose-crested, she was jaw-droppingly beautiful. Temptation personified.

Liquid brown eyes met his for a hot, heart-stopping moment before he dipped his head and explored the voluptuous curve of her breast with his mouth. The velvety skin that heated beneath his touch. Cupping her in his hand, he absorbed the contrast of her creamy skin against his darker olive complexion, fascinated by the play of dark and light, before he lowered his head to take the rosy peak into his mouth. Her back arched, her hands planting into the marble counter behind her, as she gave herself up to his exploration. Which only inflamed him further.

A whisper of a breeze floating over them, the hot, sultry air a teasing caress across his skin, he took her deeper into the heat of his mouth. Sucked the rosy nub into a hard, sensitized peak, while he rolled her other nipple between his fingers. When he was satisfied he'd given her maximum pleasure, he devoted his attention to the other firm peak, the light scrape of his teeth across the engorged flesh pulling a low, thready sound from her throat that fired his blood.

Every ounce of his blood fled south, hardening him like rock. She was the sexiest, most responsive woman he'd ever touched. Voluptuous and perfect. Needing to have her closer, driven to explore more of her perfect, silky skin, he ran his hands up the insides of her whisper-soft thighs. Dipped his palms beneath the hem of her shorts and cupped her bottom in his hands, pulling her even closer. Held her there while he dropped his mouth back to hers and devoured her in a hot, all-consuming kiss that telegraphed his hunger for her.

He was burning up for her. Somehow it penetrated his lust-soaked brain that if they kept this up, they would be having sex on the counter, consummating this insanity between them, where anyone in the household could walk in on them at any moment. The utter lapse of rationality leached into his brain, as unwelcome as it was unbidden. "Jensen—" he murmured, dragging his mouth from hers. "I don't think this is—"

Her hot, passion-soaked gaze was cloudy with desire as she struggled to understand his words. She blinked long, velvety lashes, her hands pressing against his chest to steady herself as she sought equilibrium. Liquid desire morphed into realization in those luminous, dark eyes. At what they had been about to do—ruddy color staining her cheeks. She went stiff beneath his hands, inhaling a visible breath. Then she pressed her palms harder against his chest to put distance between them.

"Jensen," he said softly, reading the regret on her face. *"Cara—"*

Jensen slid off the counter and took an unsteady step backward. Pressed her fingers to her mouth. What *was* she doing? She had nearly given herself to Cristiano on the kitchen counter. Had been so caught up in him she'd literally thrown herself at him. *Fallen into him.* She wasn't sure what was worse, her completely uninhibited response or the fact that he'd had the sense to put a stop to it and she hadn't.

What had she been thinking? How had she stepped so completely across the line? She would blame it on the late-night hour, on the intimacy of the situation, but she couldn't spin that lie even to herself. This had been building between them all week. He had simply made her go up in flames. Which was everything she'd promised herself she wouldn't do with her reputation, with her career on the line.

"This was a mistake," she bit out. "It shouldn't have happened."

"But it did," he murmured, taking a step closer. "I think both of us knew it was inevitable. I wasn't pushing you away, Jensen, I was instilling some rationality into the situation."

Inevitable? Her reckless, careless side might agree with that assessment, but the sensible, cautionary side that needed to take precedence at the moment rejected that assessment wholeheartedly. He probably thought this was normal for her, seducing a man in his kitchen. That she'd left a list of castoffs around the globe— Mata Hari incarnate. When in reality, it couldn't be further from the truth.

She hadn't had a serious relationship since Daniel, who'd unceremoniously dumped her three years ago and broken her heart. Hadn't dated anyone in Lord knew how long. Cristiano, however, had made it clear he'd bought into her headlines. And really, that wasn't such a bad thing at this point, because the smartest thing to do would be to declare this the insanity it had been and forget it had ever happened.

She was stronger than this. She *would* be stronger than this. Because everything depended on it.

"It won't happen again," she stated, in a voice filled with conviction.

"Jensen." Cristiano's gaze darkened as he stepped toward her.

She held up a hand. Stopped him in his tracks. "We both know this is a bad idea. Better to end it right here. Because tomorrow we *will* regret it."

Turning on her heel, she walked out of the kitchen and into the warm summer night.

CHAPTER FIVE

"Oh my goodness." The words slipped from Jensen's mouth, half gasp, half sigh, as she and Ilaria found themselves standing in front of *the* dress—the one that had made Francesco famous, worn in the seventies by one of the original supermodels, Isabella Müller.

They'd been cataloging the designs for the anniversary party dress auction in an afternoon that had been a bit like a dream for Jensen. Never had she imagined she would ever be in the same room as Isabella—her idol—let alone walk a runway with her. That she would be closing the show in Francesco's stunning midnight-blue couture gown he'd created for her before he'd died, which might be more beautiful than all of them.

Ilaria smiled and ran a finger down the gossamer fabric of the stunning metallic silk dress. "It's gorgeous," she murmured. "*She's* still gorgeous. I couldn't believe it when she walked into the room. It's as if she's sailed through time, un-scathed, except for a fine line or two."

Jensen attempted to quell the butterflies flut-tering in her stomach. She hoped her own career would prove as resilient as Isabella's.

But right now, her only focus was on deliver-ing for Francesco Vitale, as she'd promised she would. Justifying the trust Cristiano had placed in her. Which had involved *not* thinking about that kiss they'd shared in the kitchen, as she'd navigated the various public appearances and meetings they'd done together since, necessary collisions she'd treated with a fearsome deter-mination to ignore it all. How *unwise* the whole thing had been. How unbalanced it had made her feel. How unforgettable it was proving to be—no matter how hard she tried.

Cristiano, apparently, had decided the same thing. Not once had he addressed the chemistry still pulsing between them. The palpable ten-sion. He'd simply focused on business, polite in his usual, cordial way during the interactions they'd had. Which might sting a little, given what had taken place between them. Which was simply lust, she lectured herself sternly.

And wasn't she used to that anyway? Men desiring her, then deciding they didn't want her after all? She'd taught herself not to care. To protect herself against that hurt. This time would be no different. Except, she acknowledged, it did hurt that he'd seemingly turned things off between them. Which was ridiculous, because she'd asked for it.

She made a note of the gown Isabella would wear in her notebook, and they walked back to the front of the studio to chat through the following night's wrap party, designed to thank everyone who'd worked on the shoot and commercial for their hard work. They were just about through when Cristiano walked into the room, a distracted look on his face, a sheaf of papers in his hand, his sister's name on his lips.

His gaze flicked to Jensen, perched on a table with her notebook in hand, then back to his sister. *"Mi dispiace,"* he murmured. "I didn't realize you were busy."

"We're just finalizing some details for tomorrow night." Ilaria said. "Are you joining us? It will be nice for everyone to blow off some steam. Get some appreciation for their efforts."

A frown twisted his dark brow. "I'm going to try. I have a dinner thing. Maybe afterward." He shifted his attention to Jensen, his sapphire gaze moving over her face, taking in the pencil she had perched between her teeth, her thinking cap on. His perusal lingered on the lush, full line of her mouth for a moment longer than it should have, that electric attraction sparking between them on a wave of powerful energy, before he seemed to catch himself and moved on, scrutinizing the lines of fatigue dug into the sides of her mouth and eyes. "You look tired," he said. "Have you taken on too much?"

She shook her head, absorbing the air of intensity that emanated from him. The barely leashed energy he seemed to wear like a glove. "I'm having fun. I think you're going to be very happy with how this turns out."

"She's being modest," Ilaria interjected. "She's a genius. She has all the models doing teaser videos with clues in them that hint at Isabella's appearance. It's creating a ton of buzz online."

"Bene," he murmured, a tired smile twisting his mouth. "I like it when things fall into place. That's good to hear."

His cell phone pealed from his jacket pocket, commanding his attention. Muttering a goodbye to both of them, he left the room, a blur of dark, purposeful motion. Ilaria moved her gaze from the door back to Jensen, a curious look on her face. "Is there something going on between the two of you?"

Jensen dug her teeth into her lip. "No, why?" she said as casually as she could manage, because there wasn't, was there, really?

"Because the tension between you two is

palpable every time you're in a room together. And that dance at the Associazione Nazionale della Moda Italiana party?" She hiked a brow. "I wasn't the only one who noticed. It was fairly electric."

Jensen shrugged a shoulder. "We strike sparks off each other, that's all. Besides," she added, unable to help herself, "he belongs to Alessandra, doesn't he?"

Ilaria's azure gaze turned speculative, making Jensen instantly regret her words. "To be honest, I thought he'd have already pulled the trigger on that one. She's a perfect fit for him. Our families go way back. But," she said, hiking a shoulder, "something seems to be holding him back. Maybe he's too busy. Or maybe he's decided it isn't going to work. Which would throw off a lot of people's plans," she conceded with a wry smile. "My family has its heart set on it."

Yet another reminder that the decision she'd made to walk away from him had been the right one. That she would be setting herself up for a fall if she perpetuated this thing with Cristiano—this fairly wild attraction they shared. That the best thing she could do was pretend that kiss had never happened.

She pushed her attention back to the plans for the following evening, intent on avoiding the subject entirely. "Right," she said crisply. "So, what do we have left?"

Cristiano arrived at the wrap party when it was well under way, the crew who'd shot the campaign and commercial, as well as the cast and models, enjoying drinks and hors d'oeuvres in the gardens surrounding the villa. His dinner meeting having wrapped at a reasonable hour, his mind and body tapped out with the exhaustion searing his bones, his deal with Zhang well in hand, he'd decided to take his sister's advice and put in an appearance at the party. Demonstrate leadership at a crucial time for the company.

He stripped off his jacket and slipped into the crowd, where drink and laughter flowed liberally, a buoyant mood to the festivities, and found Antonio Braga standing beside the director of the commercial, famed Italian filmmaker Claudio Uberti.

"Perfect timing," his CMO murmured. "We've put together a rough cut of the spot. It's brilliant." An amused glitter lit his dark expression. "We couldn't have written the script any better given the current headlines. She's amazing."

Cristiano would gladly have sacrificed the sensational headlines Jensen had been generating in lieu of a more stable brand image, but he couldn't deny the synergy between the plot-line of the commercial they'd developed and the real-life drama of the face of his brand. The concept for the spot a house party being thrown by Jensen at her parents' luxurious villa while they were out of town for the weekend. The Vitale villa, with its sumptuous, elegant interior and massive chandeliers, had been, much to Filomena's dismay, used to film the spot.

As the sun slipped in a fiery ball behind the mountains, the director rolled the spot, which began with the aftereffects of the party filmed from outside the villa, with Jensen's come-hither red dress strewn across one of the manicured hedges that lined the front walkway. As the camera panned inside the villa, partygoers were sprawled asleep on every available surface—chaise longues, reading chairs, the gleaming *seminato alla veneziana* marble floors—streamers and confetti covering everything, a partygoer even asleep in the historic fountain in the backyard.

As the camera panned through the elegant splendor of the villa, various guests began to wake up in a stupor. Then came a scene of Jensen passed out in a king-size bed in the master bedroom, her current *amante* beside her, a dream she was having playing in her head—her father advising her that they would be back on Sunday afternoon. *No parties allowed.*

At that moment, Jensen's big dog, asleep beside them on the bed, nosed her awake, and she awoke in terror. Down the stairs she ran, clad in a flimsy piece of coffee-colored FV lingerie, over the gleaming marble, waking all of the partygoers in a frantic attempt to put the house back in order before her parents returned. Confetti and streamers were plucked from every available surface and tossed into bags, bottles swept into the trash and furniture shifted back to its customary position, just in time for her parents return in a sleek black helicopter.

It seemed as if she had actually managed to pull it off when her parents stepped through the Venetian glass front doors, her mother resplendent in a Pascal Ferrari suit. Until her eagle-eyed father spied a piece of confetti streaming from the massive chandelier in the entranceway, his eyes going black, and Jensen's partygoing ways were revealed.

Laughter filled the crowd at the spot's understated brilliance, a series of cheers going up for the director. Claudio took a bow, a beaming smile on his face. "Your idea to bring Jensen here was brilliant," Antonio murmured, as the crowd held up a glass for Claudio. "She is focused. At her best. Everything I imagined she could be. *Grazie mille,* Cristiano."

He wished he could say he felt the same. That he thought bringing Jensen here had been a good idea. Instead, he seemed to be more distracted with his wayward charge with every moment that passed. Watching her this past couple of weeks, he could see the consummate professional she was, completely at odds with her reckless behavior of late. The brilliant business brain she possessed. The dedication for the brand she exuded. Which had, apparently, been sideswiped by her insane schedule he'd taken charge of.

And perhaps that was all it had been. Perhaps she had simply been overwhelmed with everything on her plate, just as she'd said, and fallen back into old habits. Made some bad decisions. And perhaps, he conceded, that was simply what he wanted to believe, because he was starting to feel something for her. Something he didn't want to admit. Something he'd wanted to pursue ever since that night in the kitchen.

He spotted her at the center of a group of models, dressed in Pascal's outrageous, reckless glittering red dress. Halter-neck in style, it hugged her sensational body like a second skin, ending a few inches above the knee to show off her incredible legs. Done in a gauzy, semitransparent material, it did not take much of his imagination to envision her without it. Those decadent curves he'd explored in the kitchen.

They haunted him in his dreams. Visited him in his waking moments, too. He had the fatalistic realization they weren't going anywhere. That whatever attraction had sparked between them that night in London, whatever he had told himself about ignoring it, fighting it wasn't working. It was only making it worse. Because as unwise as it was, as irrational as he knew it to be, he wanted to know more of her. He wanted *her*.

His gaze met hers across the crowded garden, her hair a dark velvet curtain in the muted lighting, her eyes exotic ebony orbs framed by decadently long lashes, her honey-hued skin vibrant, as if lit from within. She was every bit the sparkling party girl depicted in the commercial. Every bit the wild card he'd pegged her. But she had far greater depth than anyone gave her credit for, complex, vulnerable depths that went way beneath the dazzling packaging to the intelligent, whip-sharp woman beneath. It intrigued him in a way that was approaching irresistible.

A moment passed between them, shocking in its intensity, a transfer of energy that rocked him back on his heels, it was so much bigger than both of them. He watched her almond-shaped eyes widen, before she swallowed hard, her slim throat constricting. And then her attention was claimed by someone in the crowd, and she turned and severed the connection, the regret that lanced through him tangible.

Jensen swallowed hard, attempting to absorb the energy that had passed between her and Cristiano, that had literally frozen her to the spot where she'd been standing, but the constriction in her throat was so seemingly immovable, she took a sip of her drink instead, the sparkling soda water infused with a splash of lime moistening her parched throat so that she could actually swallow.

She was exhausted from a sixteen-hour day on her feet. Back-to-back days of the same. It had taken them three hours to nail that final shot on the terrace, working against the clock as the light had faded, everything that could go wrong having gone wrong, blowing the schedule completely. Her feet were hurting in the killer five-inch heels and all she wanted to do was get out of the close-fitting dress and into her bikini, then head straight for the pool for a refreshing swim, which would make everything feel better.

Despite her mythical reputation, she was not in the business of stealing anyone's future husband, of breaking up Italian dynasties or challenging Cristiano's honor, not when the world already believed the worst of her. That she had been the catalyst behind Alexandre and Juliana's royal breakup and the resulting calamity which had ensued. Destroying one national fantasy was enough for the calendar year. This one she would leave alone.

Making the requisite rounds of the party, thanking everyone who'd done their part to make the commercial a success, she slipped quietly out of the crowd as the party was beginning to break up and down to the pool house, where she changed into an orchid-pink bikini. Securing her hair in a high ponytail, she scoured her face clean of her camera makeup before padding outside to the spotlit pool, glittering a deep cerulean blue on a perfect Italian night, the only sound on the still evening air the peaceful trickle of the waterfall at the far end of the butterfly-shaped pool.

Dipping a toe into the cool, refreshing water, she tested the temperature before wading in, allowing the water to carry away the grime and hard work of the day and ease her sore muscles. Floating silently on her back, soaking up the paradise she was in, the scent of jasmine and peony filled her head, the sky a blanket of sparkling gold stars overhead. She was in a dreamlike, half-awake, half-asleep state when the sound of clinking crystal broke the silence.

Flipping over, she tread water, her gaze widening at the figure standing on the pool deck. Cristiano, clad in navy-blue-and-green-striped swim trunks, set a bottle of champagne and two glasses he was carrying down on the tiled surface of the pool deck. Her throat, already dry from the blazing heat, went to desert dust.

She'd worked all day with a famous male model who'd been sashaying around half-naked during the out-of-control house party they'd thrown, and not once had she looked twice at his lean, well-built body. Cristiano, however, was a whole different story. All hard-packed muscle, underscored by the perfectly cut walls of his abs, a delicious vee forged a descent to his lean, powerful hips. Which were accented by muscular, trim legs that had clearly logged a great deal of miles on the cross-estate run he did every morning. The ideal combination of brawn and stealth, innate grace, which allowed him to wear his beautifully cut clothes so perfectly.

Except he didn't have many clothes on right now, she registered, her throat going even drier as she took in the low-slung dark swim trunks, which rode his lean, graceful hips. He was *insane. Spectacular.* Millie would be having a coronary right about now.

"You don't usually swim at this time of night," she managed, the words coming out as half sentence, half croak.

"You are supposed to alert someone when you are using the pool," he stated in that low, husky, accent-affecting tone that sent goose bumps to every inch of her skin.

"Yes, well," she prevaricated, "everyone was busy cleaning up from the party. I was just taking a quick dip."

"It doesn't change the rules." She could see from the stern look on his face that he wasn't kidding. And, given the rumors she'd heard about his parents' untimely death on the famous lake a few hundred feet below them, she could understand the reasoning behind the autocratic set of rules he'd thrown at her upon their arrival.

Which left only his supreme arrogance as her source of antagonism between them, and that wasn't holding up very well as the days had passed and she'd watched how hard he'd been working to make his dream for FV a reality. To systematically bring the vision he'd promised the world to life, all of the responsibility he bore to his family sitting squarely on his broad shoulders.

"Your parents died in a boating accident," she observed quietly, as he uncorked the champagne and poured it into two glasses, the froth reaching up to the rims.

"When I was fourteen, *si*." He carried the glasses to the edge of the pool, set them on the edge, then stepped down into the water, rivulets of moisture rolling off his hard-packed abs. What might have been a humiliating form of drool moistened her mouth. *Good God.* She swallowed it back. Lifted her gaze to his sapphire-blue one as he lounged back against the side of the pool opposite her. Which didn't necessarily help, as she read the banked heat gleaming there, mirroring what was bubbling up inside of her at an alarming rate.

"That must have been very traumatic," she murmured, determined to ignore it. *Desperate* to ignore it. To focus on more sobering things, such as the loss of his parents at such a young age, which must have had such an impact on him.

"It was…*difficult*." A dark light flickered in his blue gaze. "But you weather it and move on. My grandparents needed me. My sister needed me. You do what you need to do."

Which had been to protect his vulnerable young sister and eventually, to save the company his grandfather had founded. His legacy. Which once more underscored the impenetrable stuff this man was made of. Explained the rigid control with which he exerted that authority. The loyalty and duty that drove him.

She'd never met a man like him before. Her own father was so far from that type of man it was laughable, the way he'd abandoned their family without a backward glance, leaving her mother devastated and in tatters. It made her wonder, just for a second, what it would be like to be wanted by someone like him—someone so strong and honorable. Not just physically, because she knew they shared that devastating chemistry. But *emotionally*. Unconditionally.

How safe you would feel. How buffeted against the world. She imagined it would feel... *life-changing*.

But he wasn't hers to have. He would eventually be someone else's. And that, she had to keep reminding herself of.

He picked up the two glasses and handed her one.

She wrapped her fingers around the glass. Cocked a brow. "Champagne?"

"I thought we could celebrate wrapping the campaign. You did a spectacular job on it. *Grazie mille*, Jensen."

His rich, deep voice, laced with that undeniably sexy, husky accent warmed something deep inside her. And it wasn't all professional pride, because she was sure he didn't celebrate like this with all his employees. *This* was something else entirely.

She shrugged a shoulder, attempting a nonchalance she didn't remotely feel. "I was just doing my job. Working with Pascal and Claudio was a dream. I'm the lucky one."

"Well, you were brilliant," he murmured. "The marketing team is over the moon. Not to mention the assistance you've been with Federico. We pulled the Kyra campaign and showed it to him. He was very impressed. So much so that he is warming to the idea of allowing Nicholas some creative control. Which is a much more flexible stance than he's had thus far."

"That's great." She was happy her advice had helped. "I knew he would like that campaign."

"He did. Ilaria," he added, "is also ecstatic with your buzz campaign for the anniversary party. *Saluti*," he murmured, lifting his glass. "To all of your hard work."

She raised her glass, attempting to control the wild butterflies beating circular tracks through her stomach. "Aren't you afraid I might get wild?" she quipped, in an attempt to break the intensity between them. "Out of *control*?"

His sapphire gaze darkened with amusement. "I'm not so sure about that depiction of you anymore. You were drinking soda water at the party. Nor have you drunk much of anything on any social occasion we've attended since you've been here. Which leads me to believe that *partying* might not be your natural state of existence."

Her lashes drifted down, shielding her from his inscrutable assessment. "And what do you think is?"

"I don't know," he said quietly. "I think it's buried somewhere beneath those numerous impenetrable layers of yours. Those pieces of you that you refuse to show the world. You are so much more than that, Jensen."

"Perhaps," she agreed with a self-conscious shrug. "And perhaps there isn't that much more to tell."

"I think there is." He levered himself away from the wall with the push of a powerful bicep, propelling himself to within an inch or two of her. She felt a rush of blood in her ears as the force of the attraction between them roared to life, the heat of his muscular body so close she could feel it emanating from him.

"You are a brilliant marketer," he observed, his eyes on hers. "You have an innate talent. *Incredible instincts.* You could run my marketing department with the tip of your baby finger. And yet to my knowledge, you have no formal education in business."

She shook her head. "I am self-taught. Marketing always fascinated me, right from the beginning. I would study how people reacted to the things I would post. Pinpoint the best ones, study the messaging and learn how to replicate that success." She hiked a shoulder. "It came from a genuine place within me, I think that was the key. I loved fashion. I loved helping other people find their own. People picked up on that and followed me."

He cocked a dark brow at her. "And yet you persist in allowing the world to believe that you are a glamorous party girl and nothing more."

"That's my brand," she corrected. "It sells your clothes, Cristiano. Young girls want to be that glamorous icon."

"Yet we have no idea what's underneath," he said softly. "Who the real Jensen is. I wonder what the truth is?"

"A mixture of both," she answered honestly. "I'm not so difficult to figure out. I wouldn't overthink it."

His mouth curved. "There you go again, avoiding the subject." He pointed his glass at her. "Perhaps we can try another."

"Which is?"

"I would like to discuss what happened in the kitchen."

Oh no. No. They did *not* need to do that. "I think we should ignore it," she proposed firmly. "It's been working great so far."

"No, it hasn't," he murmured. "I think we both know that. I think we need to address it, Jensen."

Her throat seized. "A-address it?" she stammered, when she'd finally yanked in some air. "What do you mean?"

"Confront it," he said softly. "Face it. Deal with it. This thing between us isn't going away. It's only getting worse. And I, for one, am done fighting it."

She swallowed hard, past the flock of butterflies in her throat. He was close, too close, and her heart was beating so hard in her chest, it was difficult to function. So she grappled for the most pressing piece of information she could find to avoid what seemed like the inevitable. "Alessandra," she breathed, her eyes on his. "I am not stepping into the middle of a relationship between you two, Cristiano. It isn't my style, as much as the media likes to paint me as Mata Hari incarnate."

He frowned, a furrow marring his handsome brow. "Alessandra? We are not together."

"But you will be," she countered, far more out of breath than she would have liked. "Everyone knows it."

"Except me," he responded silkily. "Perhaps you will provide me with the benefit of the doubt on this, *bellissima*, because I am sure I am correct. Alessandra and I broke up months ago."

She caught her lip between her teeth. "I saw you together at the party. When you went to get the car. It looked intimate, Cristiano."

The furrow in his brow deepened. "So you thought there is still something between us? That's why you walked away from me in the kitchen?"

"No." She shook her head vehemently. "I walked away from you because it was a bad idea. Which it *is*," she added quickly at the dark glitter that entered his sapphire eyes. "Alessandra is only a secondary reason."

He raked a hand through his rumpled hair. "Alessandra," he said, after a moment, "was... *emotional* the night of the party. We have tried to make things work multiple times, and yet they are not working. She seems determined to make it happen. I have my doubts it ever will."

So what was he doing with her? Entertaining himself in the meantime? *Blowing off some steam?* Because surely he would never be serious about her. She wasn't about to do that with Cristiano. Not with the depth of the feelings she already had for him, feelings that seemed to be growing exponentially stronger by the moment.

"I'm not interested in being your *plaything*,"

she murmured. "Someone you blow off some steam with when you feel like it, Cristiano."

An offended look moved across his aristocratic face. "Is that what you think I'm doing? *Blowing off some steam?*"

"Yes," she said staunchly, "I do. We are attracted to each other. That's clear. Both of us are having a difficult time controlling it. Also true. But I won't put my career in jeopardy so I can have a dalliance with you, Cristiano. It's not happening."

His brow hiked higher, the offended look on his face deepening. Setting his glass down on the side of the pool, he moved until he was so close the heat emanating from him seared her skin. "Although I am a fan of *blowing off some steam* at this very moment," he murmured darkly, "because I think we both need it, my interest in you is more than surface deep, Jensen. I *like* you. I desire you. I would like to get to know you on a deeper level, *if* you will let me in. As for your career," he tacked on evenly, "I made it clear that night in the kitchen I am capable of separating it from any personal relationship we might have."

He said that, but did he mean it, when the two were so inexplicably intertwined? Which wasn't at all an effective deterrent when she was already melting inside at his words. Dissolving into a simmering inferno of emotions she had no idea how to manage. Because Cristiano announcing his intentions toward her—serious, unapologetically stated intentions of his desire to get to know her—was as terrifying as it was beguiling. Because the last time she'd done that, the last time she'd opened herself up to someone, *trusted* someone, she'd had her heart broken. And that she could never stand. Not from Cristiano.

"I'm sorry," she said quietly, her heart hammering louder than the quietly trickling waterfall. "I didn't mean to offend you. It's just—" She raked a hand over her sleek ponytail, searching for the right words. "I'm used to men viewing me as a...*prize*. As a distraction, until they move on to something better. *Serious*. It's a lot for me to put myself out there, when it's happened so many times before."

His gaze darkened to a deep midnight blue. He reached a hand out and tugged her closer, his palm settling on the lower curve of her back. Held this close to him, against the hard, hot length of him, she felt as if she'd been zapped by an electrical wire. "Do you think," he murmured, his sapphire eyes on hers, "that I would be stepping across the line if I didn't think there was something here? Because I wouldn't, *bellissima*. Trust me."

The languid warmth spreading through her melted her bones completely. His sincerity, the heat in his blue gaze, doing something strange to her insides. "I didn't put a halt to things in the kitchen because I'd regretted what I'd done," he said huskily. "I stopped things because it was insanity to be doing what we were doing in the kitchen, where any of the staff could have come in at any moment and found us. Not because I wanted to stop, Jensen."

But now they were alone. Her frantically beating heart tattooed the message on her overstimulated senses. There wasn't a soul who would be around at this time of night.

She wanted to take a leap, to trust him, to give in to this thing between them so badly, it was a living, breathing entity inside her. Obliterated her common sense. Stripped away all her barriers, until it was only them, the heat between them and the moonlight. What seemed so utterly and completely right.

Reading her thoughts, Cristiano removed the glass from her hand, set it on the side of the pool, then cupped her jaw, lowering his dark head to hers. She whispered his name, right before he captured her mouth with his in a sensual, devastating kiss designed to seduce. And this time, she gave him full permission to do so.

Her fingers curled into the thick, coarse hair

at the base of his neck, anchoring her as she met his kiss. As meltingly slow and thorough as their first kiss had been, this was even more sensual with the warm play of the water across their skin, as hands slid against warm flesh and body parts settled against each other, the rock-solid breadth of his chest an impenetrable wall that held her steady.

When he moved his mouth to the sensitive skin at the base of her ear and sank his teeth into the tender lobe, she shivered. When he traced a fiery path lower and explored the vulnerable skin at the juncture of her neck and shoulder, she shuddered, her pulse racing beneath the intimate exploration. And when he traveled even lower and brushed the callused pads of his thumbs over the peaks of her nipples, jutting through the silky material of her swimsuit, she gasped low in her throat.

Back and forth he played her, until her nipples were hard, painful peaks, aroused by his sensual touch. Until she felt it deep inside her, stirring an aching, insistent warmth. Anxious for more, she moved closer. She felt his hands move to the tie at the base of her neck, releasing the bow, and then the fabric fell away from her heated flesh, her lush curves filling his hands. She arched back in his arms to watch him, registering the dark arousal in his gaze. The reverent way he cupped her paler flesh in his hands. The way he teased the taut, rosy peaks with his fingers, igniting a firestorm of want deep inside.

"Cristiano." The need in her voice that rang out on the still night air shocked even her. Her stomach muscles went taut, clenched with need as he slid his palm down the flat surface of her abdomen to the edge of her bikini bottoms. Toyed with the flimsy edge as he took her mouth in another hot, mind-bending kiss. And then he was sliding his hand beneath the silky material and down to the tender, soft flesh at the apex of her thighs.

She moved her thighs apart on a low moan, his knowing, expert touch finding the hot, wet flesh that ached for him. His mouth on hers, he whispered sexy things to her in Italian as he stroked her from top to bottom, exploring her soft femininity, every breathy moan she made guiding his journey. And when he'd completed his survey, he set his thumb to the soft nub at the heart of her and played her in a soft, seductive motion that tore low sounds from her throat.

His name falling from her lips, she moved her hips against his hand, urging him on. And when she was writhing against him, begging for release, he slid his fingers lower and sank one inside her, sliding slow and deep. She broke the kiss, too breathless, needing air, her hips arching into the sensual, knowing caress, which went deeper with every slide, until he hit a place inside her she didn't even know existed.

Sweet, all-encompassing pleasure coursed through her, deeper than before. Even better. And when she moaned and pleaded desperately for more, he slid two of his fingers deep inside her and took the pleasure to a whole other level.

Shaking in his arms, needing release, but afraid to go there because the pleasure was so intense and she'd never felt anything so good, she rested her mouth against his cheek, gasping in a deep breath. His sensual mouth moved to her ear, his husky, accented voice a reassuring, firm command. "Let go, *cara mia*. I've got you."

Closing her eyes, her head anchored against the strong wall of his cheek, she gave in to the pleasure. Allowed the deep stroke of his big, knowing hands to catapult her over the edge into a pleasure so searing, so exquisite, she lost her breath completely. He held her through it, his fingers continuing their sensual caress until the tremors inside her had subsided.

She had barely recovered when he lifted her out of the water and placed her on the edge of the pool, his hands sweeping aside the silky material of her bikini, while his mouth found the sweet, hot flesh still reverberating from her orgasm.

His other hand tightening around the soft flesh of her hip, he held her still while he devoured her with his mouth, his intimate caresses so shockingly good, she couldn't even muster a protest. Her hands in his thick, dark hair, she rode out her release, his hot, insistent exploration sending her spiraling up the ladder of need once again, until she came apart again, her orgasm tearing through her.

So shattered she could barely breathe, she was limp and spent as he lifted her down off the ledge of the pool and into his arms, guiding her mouth back to his for a hot openmouthed kiss that shook her to her core, because she could taste herself on him, and it was the most intimate thing she'd ever experienced.

"Let's go inside," he said huskily.

She murmured her assent, unable to muster anything more coherent.

Scooping up her bikini top with his free hand, he held her against him with that awesome physical strength of his that held her in its thrall, her arms and legs wrapped around his muscular body, as he carried her out of the pool. Acquiring one of the thick towels they'd left on a lounger, he dried her off, moving the fabric over the smooth skin of her shoulders, then the rounded curves of her breasts, paying reverent attention to the rosy peaks, hard and aroused in the moonlight.

"Bellissima," he murmured.

She melted. He wrapped the towel around her, drawing her toward him, his palm splayed over the curve of her buttock as they shared a passionate, sensual kiss. It took her a full second to register the flash of light that exploded behind her head, she was so caught up in him. Cristiano, however, was faster, a dark curse leaving his mouth as he released her and set her behind him, his broad shoulders blocking her from the blinding series of lights that exploded on the night air.

Camera flashes, she registered belatedly, her stomach plunging to the ground. *Oh God.* Shoving her bikini top behind his back, Cristiano barked at her to put it on. Her hands shaking, she fumbled in her efforts, cursing herself weakly as her fingers refused to cooperate. Finally, she managed to get it on, tying it clumsily behind her back and neck. By that time, Cristiano was on his phone, issuing terse instructions to his security staff, an infuriated note to his voice.

How they had ever penetrated the ironclad perimeter of the estate, she had no clue. Unless, she registered numbly, they had somehow taken advantage of the activity surrounding the wrap party, and the various suppliers who had worked it, to slip in undetected. Which would take a sophisticated, experienced paparazzo with extensive connections.

A feeling of dread wove its way up her spine. This bore all the hallmarks of one of her mother's operations. She had the means to do it and stupidly, perhaps, even the motivation after Jensen had texted her back earlier that she was happy the campaign had wrapped and looking forward to the party to celebrate. A carrot she'd offered her mother after not replying to dozens of her texts in an attempt to stay focused. And, she conceded, a part of her had been worried about how she was doing, anticipating another one of her vicious plunges.

Oh no. Please, God, no.

Cristiano barked a final order into his phone, then slid the device into his pocket. The camera flashes had subsided, his security crew undoubtedly hot on their heels. But she knew the damage was done. The intimate sort of photos they could have taken. How disastrous this was going to be.

"I need to sort this out," he murmured, a furious look on his face. "Go inside."

"Cristiano," she murmured, desperate to say

something, *anything* that would rescue this situation before it spun out of control.

He set a palm to her back and moved her bodily inside. "Stay here. I'll find you later."

CHAPTER SIX

But Cristiano didn't find her later. Jensen waited until after midnight for him to return, and when there was still no sign of him, she finally went to bed and fell into an exhausted, restless sleep. When she woke, she was shocked to find it was eight o'clock, the sun blazing a path into the sky, and remembered she hadn't set her alarm because they'd finished shooting and she was free for the day. Which would have been lovely, if not for the disaster of the night before. What she had to face.

She picked up her phone. Checked her notifications. There were dozens. A brief scan of the headlines revealed it couldn't be good. Her heart plunged, resting somewhere above her churning, misplaced insides.

Davis Drops Prince for Fashion Magnate, read the headline of a British daily newspaper. *Caught in the Act!* blared a spicier UK tabloid.

The CEO and the Supermodel, the clever title for an Italian tabloid, known for its juicy stories.

Oh my God. Her heart dropped further, if that was possible. She clicked on the first story, from the gossip page of one of Britain's daily newspapers. Below the headline was a story suggesting she'd left Alexandre for Cristiano, in a fortuitous swap, alongside an intimate shot of them in the pool together, her wrapped in his arms, locked in a passionate kiss. Which was likely as racy as the newspaper had been willing to go. The tabloids, on the other hand, had no such scruples.

She opened the British tabloid, known for its scandalous coverage, terrified at what she'd read. Under the headline *Caught in the Act!* were two photos, one of her and Cristiano on the dance floor from the Associazione Nazionale della Moda Italiana party, suggesting speculation had been rife about their relationship ever since the intimate dance at the party. Beside it was a photo of Cristiano carrying her out of the pool the night before, minus her bikini top. His arm was shielding her nudity from the camera, but her half-clothed state was apparent, as was the fact that they only had eyes for each other.

Her heart went into a free fall. This couldn't be happening. Not now. Not when everything had been going so well. When she'd been doing her job exactly as Cristiano had mandated, when the scandalous headlines about Alexandre had dissipated and the campaign was set to be a brilliant success. When Cristiano had said those monumental things to her last night about wanting to get to know her. About wanting *her*.

Her stomach churned, bile rising hot and insistent in her throat. Her mother had done this. She was sure of it. That she would do this to her, take advantage of her like this, despite her explicit instructions to leave her alone, was a betrayal that rose above all others. She couldn't believe she'd done it. But she was more angry at herself for being naive enough to think her mother could employ that type of rationality when she was in such a desperate state. It had been a massive mistake.

She read everything so that she knew the damage that had been done, then dressed in a T-shirt and shorts, shoved her hair into a ponytail, and slipped on running shoes. Then she headed up to the villa, dread in her every step. Filomena was in the kitchen, making coffee, a delicious aroma permeating the sunny space.

"Buongiorno." She murmured a greeting. "Has he gone to the office?" she asked, not even attempting to avoid the subject, because she knew Filomena would know. Would have gotten the full report from the staff.

"He's here, in his office, on a call," the house-keeper replied. "You look like you need some coffee. Sit."

She sank down on a stool, eyes bleary. Filomena handed her a steaming cup of coffee and a pastry, but Jensen refused the croissant, her stomach churning too violently to entertain the idea of eating. She took a sip of the coffee. Eyed the housekeeper. "Has everyone seen the photos?"

"*Si.*" Filomena leaned a generous hip against the island. "It's the talk of the estate. They weren't able to catch them. They must have escaped via the water. There was so much coming and going last night, things weren't as strict as they normally are."

Jensen's head began to throb in earnest. She pressed her fingers to her temples and willed it away.

"Let's be honest," the housekeeper said quietly. "It was only a matter of time before this happened between you two."

Jensen's eyes widened. "Alessandra is not the right woman for him," the housekeeper continued, in her patented, matter-of-fact tone. "She is selfish and focused on what he can give her. You are different. He seems happy when he is around you. Which," she added, "he deserves to be."

And how was he going to feel this morning with everything blowing up in his face? Jensen's insides twisted into a ball. Because this wasn't just another scandal. This one had him at the heart of it.

"It will blow over, *piccolo mio*," Filomena said quietly. "Don't fret." She walked over to the cupboard and retrieved a bottle of painkillers and set them in front of Jensen.

Jensen had taken the painkillers and was stewing over her coffee when Cristiano walked into the kitchen a few minutes later, dressed in a crisp navy-blue suit, gingham-checked white-and-blue shirt and purple tie. Looking crisp and beautiful, in high-alert business mode, the lines of fatigue etched around his eyes and mouth were the only sign that anything was off-kilter.

His gaze moved from her to Filomena. "Give us a moment, *per favore*?"

Filomena nodded and vanished inside the massive pantry. Cristiano leaned a hip against the island. Surveyed her pallor. The bottle of painkillers in front of her. "Are you all right?"

She nodded. "Just a headache."

He rubbed his palms against his eyes. "*Mi dispiace*. I was up half the night with my communications team, attempting to stop them from publishing the photos. But we couldn't track them in time, given we didn't know who it was who took them."

Her stomach roiled. She didn't want to tell him. Would rather do anything but. But she knew who it had been. Almost assuredly.

"It was my mother, Cristiano."

He frowned. "How do you know? It could have been anyone."

"Because it has her MO written all over it." She drew in a breath. "I hadn't talked to her in a while. I'd been ignoring her texts, because I needed to stay focused and she was pressuring me into doing a follow-up stunt to the Alexandre thing and I wanted nothing to do with it. Yesterday, I texted her and checked in. Told her the campaign was wrapped and I was looking forward to the party. She clearly saw an opportunity and took it."

An incredulous look moved across his face. "She would do that to you? Hurt you in that way?"

She absorbed his disbelief. The shock written across his face. She didn't expect him to understand the way her mother's mind worked. How messed up her family was. It continued to astonish even her. Nor could she explain how desperate her mother was, because that would lead to her current addiction issues and mental health challenges and that was a place she couldn't go.

She fidgeted with the handle on her cup. "She destroyed my sister Ava's life when she convinced her to get married for the season finale of the show, when all of us knew Dimitrio was an unfaithful piece of dirt who wasn't good enough to grace the ground she walked on. But Ava loved him, it generated the highest ratings of any network reality show in the history of television, so who cared?" She threw up a hand. "The show must go on."

Cristiano stared at her, wide-eyed. Her shoulders slumped. "She thinks about it for about ten seconds, then decides we'll forgive her. I'm so sorry, Cristiano. It was a gross miscalculation on my part to trust her. It was my fault."

His gaze darkened. "It wasn't your fault. My security should have caught them. Not to mention the fact that I was the one who came down there last night with the champagne, intent on pursuing things with you. If anyone offered them the opportunity, it was me."

She scoured his face, attempting to figure out how he felt about it all, but his phone was buzzing, his attention diverted as he glanced down at it, then back up at her. "The communications team is advising we let this blow over. Let it run its course. There's no point in chasing after a horse that's already left the barn."

She knew that to be the truth.

He glanced at his watch. "I have a meeting in forty-five minutes. A crisis brewing in LA with my supply chain. I have to go."

She nodded, wishing desperately for some reassurance, for some indication of where they stood, but he merely bent his head and brushed a kiss to her cheek, then picked up his briefcase and left.

She stared down at her coffee. He had so much on his plate. So much pressure and stress, and she had only added to it with this. Done the one thing he'd asked her not to do in creating another scandal.

She knew that shuttered, aloof look. Daniel had worn it before he'd ended things between them. When he'd arrived home at their apartment, only to find a horde of paparazzi waiting, hot on another story. She couldn't even remember what it had been. She only remembered the look of finality on Daniel's face when he'd told her they were done. To pack her things and go.

She sank her teeth into her lip. Had she ruined any chance of a relationship with Cristiano? Of pursuing this fledgling connection between them, one that seemed so very monumental and different? Surely he wouldn't want anything to do with her after this?

Cristiano got into his sports car and drove the winding highway to Milan. He was cutting it close for his meeting, traffic thick on the early-morning commute, and he had a full-on crisis to navigate in LA, one he thought he'd put to bed weeks ago. Not helped by the couple of hours' sleep he was operating on, which had put him in a combustible mood. Exacerbated by the information Jensen had just given him.

Veronica Davis had sent that photographer to scale his defenses and take lurid, intimate photos of her daughter to satisfy the gossip mill of a television show she subsisted on. He was angry, *furious* about it. At Jensen's mother for abusing her daughter's confidence. For invading his privacy. At the Davis matriarch's absolute refusal to acknowledge the damage she was inflicting on her daughter and her career.

He couldn't believe she would do that to Jensen. But then again, she'd been doing it her entire life. Why stop now? It made him so angry he wanted to slap a restraining order on Veronica Davis and sue her for invading his privacy. But that wasn't going to help the situation. Not aided by the fact that he had known exactly what he was doing when he'd taken that champagne down to the pool last night to seduce Jensen. He'd chosen to complicate things by getting involved with her. By giving in to the madness that consumed him every time he was within touching distance of her.

He was the one who had provided the fodder

for her mother's cameras, the photos of Jensen and the prince in the Trevi Fountain downright innocent compared to the intimate photos of them in the pool the night before.

He'd barely been awake, without even a cup of coffee in hand, when he'd received a tearful phone call from his ex-fiancée. Which shouldn't have damn well been a thing, because he'd ended that relationship on as clear a note as he'd thought humanly possible. But Alessandra had been wrecked, *distraught*, which made him wonder if his family had been stepping in, massaging that relationship, planting the seed that he would come around eventually. Which had left him somewhere close to incendiary.

He knew the political value Alessandra brought to the company. The strategic asset she was. He'd spent his entire life devoting himself to FV and what the company needed. Alessandra would no doubt make someone the perfect wife. Just not him. Because after the passion he and Jensen had shared, he knew a marriage to Alessandra would never be enough. His head wanted her to be the one, but his heart did not. It was a truth he was finally willing to admit. His heart was in another place entirely. Which was a problem.

Jensen spent the next few days working long hours to make sure every model who was to appear in the anniversary party show knew their role, right down to the last detail. She knew how frantic the final minutes before a show could be and wanted to make sure they got it right, particularly when she'd asked each model to share a memory of her work with Francesco during the backstage video they were shooting, which she hoped would be a wonderful retrospective of his career. Not to mention the fact that if she was busy, she didn't have to think about her mother and how furious she was with her.

She'd received a text from Veronica late the day the photos had appeared, a response that had made her so angry she hadn't talked to her since.

Of course it was me, darling. It was too good an opportunity to pass up. The Alexandre story was dying out and this gives it fresh legs. Apologies, I know you wanted to keep things quiet, but the producers are ecstatic.

She'd called her sisters, smoke coming out of her ears. Strategized an intervention for when she returned to New York in a few weeks. Obviously, Veronica needed more help than she'd been getting. No longer was Jensen going to bankroll her while sacrificing her own future. Cristiano had been right. She did know herself.

Knew who she wanted to be. And she was done enabling her mother to her own detriment.

But first, she acknowledged, her hair and makeup done as the preshow buzz reached a fever-pitch backstage at the party, held at a magnificent seventeenth-century palace in the heart of Milan, she had a promise to Cristiano to keep. She had promised him tonight would be one for the history books. That she would make it the most-talked-about event of the fashion calendar, less Pascal's spectacular debut in a few days' time.

Picking up her bejeweled pink phone, she wound her way through the models, all in various states of readiness, warning them she was about to start filming.

Assured that all the models were at least partially attired in the short Vitale blue robes as she herself was, she started filming with her phone, introducing the backstage video and making her way through the buzzing crowd, stopping to speak with each notable model as they shared a reminiscence about Francesco and his career. By the time she made it to Isabella Müller, who offered a great story about the young designer's genius and his subsequent rise to stardom, it was time to sign off the video, put her phone down and change into her dress, with the show having just begun.

Her heart pumping with blood, her skin flushed with excitement, she slipped on Francesco's bold one-shoulder midnight-blue gown, with its spectacular bedazzled cutout detailing across the back, accentuated with crystal paisley embellishments. A thigh-high slit showed off her endless legs, the figure-hugging design of the dress and the silky, rich material highlighting her pert posterior, perhaps her best asset.

Her dresser adjusted the single strap of the gown so the material lay perfectly flat against her skin, like a glove. She added sparkling diamond drop earrings and a matching cuff bracelet, the perfect accompaniment to the glamorous dress. Her chestnut tresses caught up in a high ponytail, curled, sophisticated ends gave her an effortlessly chic look, highlighting her naturally striking features, set off by a hint of bronzer that dusted her impressive cheekbones.

"Are you ready?" Isabella murmured, appearing at her side, her still-strong accent giving the words an exotic flavor, her calm composure born of thousands of hours on the runway.

Jensen nodded. Wiggled her toes in the silver stilettos she'd donned in an attempt to convince herself this was really happening. That she was about to walk the runway behind her idol. It brought all of her teenage fantasies full circle, and she thought she might burst from the wonder of it all.

Tempering her unusual nerves, she followed Isabella to the wings, created tonight in the ornate anteroom of the palace gallery. The beautiful gilded room was packed with every notable face in fashion, along with every kind of celebrity imaginable, from film to music to theater to the literary world. Given the buzz she'd generated with her social media campaign, she knew it had provided an extra push, intense visibility around the night, but even she was shocked by some of the faces in attendance.

Her gaze found Cristiano, standing in the audience, leaning against a pillar that rose to the majestic second-floor balcony. Dressed in a superbly cut black suit tonight, with a snow-white shirt and a Vitale blue tie, he looked so insanely handsome, her heart skipped a beat, then galloped forward at an unsustainably quick pace.

She'd only seen him in passing since that morning in the kitchen, learning from Ilaria that he'd been embroiled in a supply chain crisis in LA that was causing serious difficulties in the manufacturing process. She'd been worrying about him, about the pressure he'd been under, about everything on his shoulders right now. But according to an earlier conversation with Ilaria, they'd had a breakthrough last night, and a temporary solution was now in place. Which was a massive relief.

"He is ridiculously handsome," Isabella murmured, following her gaze to Cristiano. "Not such a bad subject to play to, is he?"

Jensen's stomach dropped, swirling in a crazy, off-beat rhythm. She had no idea where they stood. Whether he'd changed his mind about her after the paparazzi debacle. She'd convinced herself that if he had, it would be fine. It was always fine. She would bury herself in her work and pretend she didn't care, because that's what she always did. Ignore how she felt, retreat into herself, refuse to acknowledge her feelings. Because then, she'd never have to feel the pain of rejection. Of him deciding he didn't want her after all.

But she knew she was lying to herself. Knew why she'd been running from him the past few weeks. Because of the wild, uncontrollable longing he unearthed in her. Because she wanted *him*. The strong, honorable, impenetrable man that he was, one a woman might desperately want at her back. The kind of man she never even knew existed. She wanted the headlines to be true—that she could be the woman at his side. And she thought she might be fooling herself into thinking that could ever happen. Because surely, he'd never choose someone like her.

The show director announced her cue. Drawing in a deep breath, she pushed her shoulders back and stepped into the lights at the head of the runway.

Cristiano watched Jensen step into the spotlight in Francesco's magnificent midnight-blue dress, so spectacularly beautiful, she hurt his eyes. She was the brightest star by far on a night that had featured a cavalcade of them. A spectacular celestial event you saw once in a lifetime. From her gleaming mahogany hair, swept back from her face in a high ponytail, to her ebony eyes that shone with exotic promise, to her incredible, curvaceous body set off to perfection in the stunning dress, she was a vision.

She had promised him she would deliver, and she had. Social media was ablaze with photos and posts about tonight's show, making it unlikely any moment in fashion would top it this year. She had been dedicated and brilliant these past few weeks, everything he'd needed her to be. But she'd also gone above and beyond the call of duty to make sure everything fell into place for tonight.

The relief he felt was palpable. A massive weight off his shoulders. He'd needed tonight to go perfectly and it had. A fitting tribute to his grandfather's brilliant legacy. But he knew it meant more to him than that. He'd needed to know he could depend on Jensen. That he was right about her. That his instincts had been correct. Because if he'd thought the last few days might have cooled his ardour, might somehow have imprinted some last vestige of sanity on his brain, they had instead only underscored his feelings for her. Intensified those emotions.

He had missed her. Missed her company. Missed talking to her—the escape she provided from the endless weight on his shoulders. And he wasn't in the mood to hold back. Not any longer.

She stepped back with the other models, her breathtaking trip down the runway complete, applauding the historic moment as his grandmother stepped onto the stage. Seemed utterly flustered when Marcella caught her and pressed a kiss to both of her cheeks, murmuring something in her ear that unearthed a flush across her high-boned cheeks. He hoped to hell it was the credit she deserved for her efforts.

"She is spectacular tonight," Ilaria murmured, from her position by his side. "Our brand ratings have skyrocketed since the photos of you two went public."

"I thought the Italian people were furious

with her for violating the sanctity of the Trevi Fountain."

Ilaria smiled. "The Italian press is fickle. They have decided you are far too glamorous a couple for them to resist."

Cristiano wasn't in a mood to disagree. He'd decided he wanted Jensen a long time ago. He was all in. And he didn't much care what anyone thought about it.

He bided his time. Through the three-course dinner that followed. Through the speech he made to mark his grandfather's legacy and the others that followed. Through the formal passing of the baton to Pascal, to the prescribed post-dinner chitchat Milanese society required on a gorgeous, late-summer evening. Through the results of the auction, which raised millions for charity, a mind-numbing blur of voices and niceties he abided rather than actually listened to, he was so physically exhausted, he could barely stand on two feet.

He watched Jensen flit from group to group, spreading that inexorable, undeniable charm of hers, casting everything and everyone she touched in a golden glow. Really, he had no interest in dancing when the time came, but the prospect of holding her in his arms held too great a sway. As the band swung into a slow, sultry number, the majestic frescoes of the ballroom a stunning backdrop, he moved purposefully, locating her in a group of people near the bar, giving in to the fiery need that burned in his veins.

Her back turned to him, she was cast in candlelight, the midnight-blue gown following every line of her voluptuous body in a loving, sensual caress. He thought he might be a little obsessed with her perfect backside, which undoubtedly held the entire male population in its thrall. It made him think very improper thoughts, with only her, that dress and himself starring in those particular fantasies. And maybe that was because he hadn't been able to get that night in the pool out of his head and everything in him was clamoring for them to finish what they'd started.

"Dance?" he requested huskily, tapping a finger on her shoulder and holding out a hand. Eyes smoldering with the same banked need he felt, she voiced her excuses to the group and placed her hand in his, following him to the dance floor, which was teeming with partygoers enjoying the live music under a massive twinkling chandelier.

She moved into his arms, one hand clasped in his, the other on his shoulder. He settled his palm to the curve of her hip, just beneath the enticing cutouts that exposed her bare, silky flesh, his other hand wrapping around hers. She was warm, he registered, a flush dusting the creamy perfection of her cheeks, her décolletage, above the sophisticated asymmetrical neckline of her dress.

Luminous brown eyes met blue in a gaze that lasted more than a heartbeat. "Aren't you afraid this will stoke the rumor mill? Make people talk?"

"Let them." The low timbre of his voice sent a shiver through Jensen, as Cristiano rested his sapphire gaze on hers. "Thank you for everything you've done to make tonight a success. It is everything I'd imagined it would be and more."

Jensen absorbed the dark flicker of emotion in his gaze. "You miss him."

He inclined his head. "He was everything. I wish he could have been here tonight to see this. His biggest fear was that he would be forgotten. Tonight would have obliterated that thought."

"He had no need to worry about that," she murmured. "He's one of the greatest designers of all time. *Irreplaceable*."

"*Si*. But he was human, like everyone else. He worried Pascal's legacy would supersede his."

Jensen absorbed that surprising revelation. She'd never thought of the brutally intimidating Francesco as in any way human. He had always seemed so much larger than life. And yet she could see how hard that would be, hand-picking your successor. Finding someone who could carry out your vision, who was success-ful enough on his own two feet to command the respect of the fashion world, and yet being equally afraid he could overshadow you. She had felt that fear with Ariana.

"Marcella said some very nice things to me on the runway. About tonight."

"It's about time. You've been spectacular." Cristiano's fingers tightened around her waist, drawing her closer, the tantalizing scent of his sophisticated cologne filling her head, annihi-lating her brain cells. "What was it like to close the show? To walk alongside Isabella?"

"Incredible," she breathed. "She is such an icon. I'm in awe of everything she's done. Both as a model and a businesswoman."

He inclined his head. "Her activewear line has been very successful."

She dug her teeth into her lip. "We had a really good conversation about the pressures of modeling. How she handled it. She knew it wasn't going to last forever, so she put a contin-gency plan in place. Developed the idea for the activewear line while she was still modeling. Leveraged her influencer status to do it. Someday—" she said, her teeth sinking deeper into her lip "—I'd like to follow in her footsteps."

Cristiano cocked a dark brow at her. "How so?"

"I've always been good at makeup. I helped the team with the shoot when we were down a person and they loved the work I did. I'm always doing experimental videos on social media that get lots of views. I thought," she said, feeling more than a little awkward at exposing her inner musings, because she'd always been afraid they would be shot down given the criticism she'd faced, "I would like to create my own makeup line. If I could find the right partner."

He must have heard the self-consciousness in her voice, because his sapphire gaze softened to a deep midnight blue. "I think that could only be a rip-roaring success. Not only do you have the sharpest business brain of anyone I know, but you have the personality and charm to sell sunshine to a Sicilian, *cara*. Ilaria showed me one of your how-to videos. I think it had garnered about three million views."

A dark flush lit her cheeks. Both at the compliment and the endearment he'd thrown so casually at her. Except Cristiano never did anything carelessly; he did it with thought and *intention*, and the realization sent a full-body shiver through her.

"If you like," he murmured, drawing her closer still, his eyes on hers, "I will put you in contact with a friend who runs a global cosmetics brand. You can decide if it's something you want to pursue. But for now," he said, his mouth moving to her ear, "I am done talking business. I am done solving global supply chain crises, and I am definitely done pretending I don't want you, when I so clearly do."

Jensen's knees sagged, zapped by that definitive promise. "Cristiano," she breathed.

He didn't reply. Just slid his palm lower, until it was resting against the bare skin of her lower back, his fingertips burning her flesh like a brand. A promise. They stopped talking then, just danced, the way they moved together an instinctive thing now. As if their bodies recognized each other in some primal, perfect connection that defied reason. Definition.

"I meant what I said in that pool, Jensen. I'm not walking away from you. I want to know you," he murmured. "All of you. But if I am going to do that, you have to let me in. You have to let me know all of you. You have to trust me."

Her heart raced in her chest. Because hadn't that always been her biggest fear? That if she shared herself with someone, *truly* shared herself with someone, if she let them beneath the sparkly outer packaging she had always hidden behind, they wouldn't want her anymore? They might reject her like everyone else had done in her life. Declare her as superficial as the world believed her to be. And that she could not bear, not from Cristiano.

But if she never learned to open up, to make herself vulnerable, how would she ever know what she could have with him? What she was capable of? If she could have that relationship with him she wanted so desperately? Because she did. There was no point in denying it anymore.

"I am scared," she murmured breathlessly. "I don't know if I can do it, Cristiano. I've never opened up to anyone like that. I've never *allowed* myself to open up like that, because for me, it's always meant getting hurt."

His eyes glittered a deep sapphire blue. "I won't hurt you, *mia cara*. I promise you that."

He bent his head and kissed her, a deep, soul-affirming caress that stole her breath. As if they weren't in the middle of a room full of people. As if he didn't care who knew how he felt about her. It disassembled something deep inside her. Broke down her walls. *Shattered* them.

She kissed him back, her fingers tangling in the coarse hair at the base of his nape. Moved closer still, until she could feel the steady beat of his heart against hers. The heat of his tall, strong body transferring itself to her. Dimly aware of flashbulbs going off around them, she couldn't bring herself to care, she was so lost in him. In how he made her feel.

They danced like that for a while, reveling in the heat. The anticipation. His hand on her hip moved lower, bringing her into closer contact with the lower half of his body. A gasp left her throat. He was hard and aroused and oh so impressive and it made her heart pound in her chest.

"I think it's time to leave. *Sei d'accordo?*"

She nodded her head, wordlessly. Somehow fumbled her way through the good-nights they quickly made before heading for the exit, where Cristiano's driver was waiting. Climbing into the back of the luxurious vehicle, she had barely registered the click of the door before he was reaching for her, the privacy panel shielding them from view.

Straddling his hard, sinewy thighs, she framed his face with her palms. Lowered her mouth to his. The kiss they shared was passionate and urgent. Long, leisurely slides of her mouth against his hard, sensual one, exchanging breath on heady murmurs that devolved into a more intimate exploration of each other involving a delicate slide of her tongue against his, then his against hers, his knowing expertise lighting her body on fire.

Unable or unwilling to call a halt to the passionate exchange, she dug her fingers into the knot of his tie, breaking the kiss for a moment of air while she stripped it off and tossed it on the seat of the car. Fingers stumbling over the buttons of his snow-white shirt, she managed to get it open, her mouth sliding down over his jaw to explore his salty, masculine skin, dusted with a light covering of coarse dark hair. Slid her hands over the magnificent definition of his muscles as they converged at the center of his hot, hard abdomen, not an ounce of additional flesh on him.

He was so masculine, so intoxicating to her senses, that her brain was overwhelmed. Overstimulated. *Overcome.* He muttered something in Italian, his palms cupping her bottom in the glittery dress. Dragging her closer, so she was straddling the hard jut of his erection. So she could feel every impressive inch of him imprinted beneath the fine material of his trousers, branding her, promising heaven.

Her hands dropped, fumbling with the button on his trousers. She wanted, *needed* him inside her. Needed to feel him filling her with that awesome power of his. To finally consummate this wild thing between them. But he clamped his fingers over hers and dragged her hand away.

"Not here," he rasped.

She yanked in a centering breath as he set her back on the seat, composed himself, his hands dealing with the buttons on his shirt, then depressed the privacy screen enough to tell the driver to step on it, before they lapsed into an anticipation-fueled silence that stoked her nerves to a fever pitch.

The villa was cast in a muted glow when they pulled up in the circular drive. Cristiano issued a curt thank-you to his driver, set his palm to her back and ushered her inside and up the magnificent staircase to the master suite.

With its warm Lombardy cotto stone floors, antique Venetian chandeliers and glorious views of the mountains beyond the open French doors, it was heavenly. She'd fallen in love with the space when they'd shot the television commercial, drawn to its sumptuous elegance and warmth. But now, with the elegant sconces on the wall casting a golden glow throughout the space, the harvest moon gleaming a glorious pink and orange through the open windows, she felt as if she didn't have enough air in her lungs.

Or maybe it was Cristiano, his jacket discarded, in the dove-white shirt, open at the throat to reveal his deep olive skin, his hands tossing his gold cuff links on a dresser. He made her heart flutter in her chest.

"Take the dress off," he murmured, his huskily issued command singeing her blood.

With anyone else, she might have hesitated, felt self-conscious. But not with Cristiano. She moved her shaking fingers to the side zipper of the dress, sliding it down, until it reached its mooring, his hot gaze following every movement. Sinking her fingers into the shimmery fabric, she pulled the dress up and over her head and threw it on a chair, standing in front of him, clad in a wispy cream thong and matching bra.

"Come here." His deep midnight-blue gaze seared her skin. Heart slamming in her chest, her breath coming in short, uneven pulls of air, she closed the distance between them. Stopped when she was mere centimeters from him. He raised his hand, ran his thumb along the smooth skin beneath the clasp of her bra and unhooked it with an expertise that stoked the nerves raging inside her.

When he was done, he sat down on the edge of the massive king-size bed, caught her hand in his and drew her forward, until she was kneeling on the bed, straddling his hard thighs, his palm at her back steadying her. His slumberous gaze fixed on her pert, uplifted breasts, the hazy desire shimmering in his dark blue eyes igniting a confidence she sorely needed.

Closing her eyes, she absorbed the searing pleasure as he took one rosy peak inside his mouth and caressed her, bolts of sensation arcing from the sensitive tip to somewhere deep inside, lighting her on fire. It was so good, so intense, it made her moan, dig her fingernails into the skin at the nape of his neck and move needily against the hard ridge of him beneath his trousers, her thin panties little barrier as she rocked against him, each breathy movement pushing the tension between them higher.

His blue gaze tangled with hers as anticipation tore the air between them. Then he took the other throbbing peak inside the heat of his mouth, taking his time, making sure she felt all of it, making sure she was molten for him inside, ready to internally combust, before he rolled her beneath him, sank his fingers into the delicate strings of her panties and stripped them off of her, so she was bare beneath him. Vulnerable. Aching. Wanting.

She reached for him, attempting to relieve him of his clothes, because he still had far too many on, but his knees on the inside of her thighs spread her open instead, the extreme vulnerability of her position halting her protest in her throat. Dipping his head, he trailed his mouth and tongue from the dip of her belly button to the jut of her hip bone, then lower, until she could feel the warm heat of his breath on her aroused flesh seconds before he consumed her with one possessive lap of his tongue, his palm on her belly, holding her where he wanted her when she bucked up from the pleasure of it. Eyes on hers, his gaze hot, he murmured sexy Italian words to her while he consumed her, words she had no idea of the meaning of, except that she wanted more of what he was giving her.

Sinking her fingers into his thick, coarse hair, she held him there while he feasted on her, driving her higher with every expert caress designed to make her mad. Until she was shaking, quivering, her entire body poised on an earth-shattering precipice. Then he kicked her over it with ruthless precision, the hard lash of his tongue against the trembling, tender nub at the heart of her sending a violent wave of pleasure to every nerve ending in her body, in a release that seemed to go on forever.

Cristiano stripped off his clothes, his eyes never leaving the woman in his bed, her chestnut-colored hair a dark flame against the ivory sheets, her long, golden limbs splayed out, his for the taking. She watched as he shrugged the shirt off his broad shoulders, pushed his trousers and boxers over his hips, sheathed himself, then prowled back to the bed to join her.

He was hard, aching for her. He was fairly sure he'd never wanted anything this much in his life. He was also fairly sure she felt the same. Although she was doing her best to maintain her cool, those liquid ebony eyes of hers flashing with heat and humor as he set a knee on the bed and came down over her.

"I will say, that might have been worth the wait," she murmured, her teeth lodging in her full bottom lip.

He slid a palm down the velvety surface of her thigh and urged it around his waist. Slid his other hand to the silky, slick flesh at the apex of her thighs, his thumb finding the tiny nub that gave her pleasure. A moan left her throat, her even white teeth sinking deeper into her lush lip at his slow, sensual caress, her ebony eyes darkening to black.

"Might?" he murmured softly, "I think we're going to need a more resounding response on that one."

Jensen would have told him just about anything if he'd keep touching her like he was, his teasing, circular caresses winding her up all over again, as if he hadn't just given her one of the best orgasms of her life, still pulsing through her nerve endings. But then he slid his middle finger, slick from touching her, inside her pulsing flesh in a smooth, velvet stroke and she arched into the caress, another low moan escaping her mouth. A few deep, even plunges that felt like heaven, then that teasing circular motion of his thumb against her clitoris again, a ghostly sweet caress, and then a second finger sliding inside her, stretching her velvet heat.

"Cristiano…" she breathed, eyes on his. "Please."

"Please, what?"

"Please—I need you. I need—"

He brought his mouth down to hers. *Tell me.*

"There is no…*might*. It's so good. Please—"

He slid his palm under the satiny smooth skin of her buttocks. Raised her up so he could enter her on a swift, firm thrust. She gasped as he pushed his way inside her, filling her inch by inch with his thick, hard length, his hand at her hip controlling the movement with a sensual expertise that stole her breath. He was so big, so *overwhelming*, her body had to adjust, softening with each lazy stroke to accommodate him, until finally, he was buried inside her and she was struggling for air.

"Breathe," he murmured, his gaze on hers.

Erotic whispers shivered across her skin as she did as he commanded. Felt the pulse of his heartbeat buried deep inside of her, an achingly intimate connection she felt all the way to her soul. Slowly, inexorably, her body adjusted to his. Melted around his possession. And when his hands tightened around her hips and he started to move, holding her still as he stroked up deep inside her, so thick and masculine he stretched her completely, she knew it would never be like this with anyone else. This mind-numbingly good. This soul-shattering.

Drawing his mouth down to hers, she kissed him, her nails scraping down the hard muscles of his back, each hard stroke melting her insides to liquid and deepening his dominant possession. Until she was completely his. And when he curved his fingers around her thigh and wrapped it around his waist, his palm raising her bottom so he could hit a sweet spot, an angle that promised ecstasy, a scream ripped from her throat and shattered the night air as they came together in a hot rush of pleasure that made the whole room go black.

CHAPTER SEVEN

CRISTIANO ARRIVED HOME well after seven, exhausted from an hours-long meeting with his lawyers in which they'd attempted to work through the red tape surrounding his deal with Nicholas Zhang, set to close as soon as they'd manage to do so. It was a relief, given the stakes he was gambling with. But it still didn't mean he hadn't pushed the company to the brink, that every piece of his complex, multifaceted plan had to go as envisioned or it could and would come tumbling down around him. A pressure that coiled around his neck like a golden noose.

With hours of work still left to do, he retreated to his office, requested more strong coffee from Filomena, and attempted to revive his brain, which refused to work on the few hours' sleep he'd had over the past week. Avoided the fact that Jensen was home this evening, and just a stone's throw away, a respite he had allowed himself far too many times this past week, because it felt like the actions of a drowning man, grabbing hold of a lifeline. A foreign vulnerability he had no idea how to process, because it felt like weakness—a state of affairs he avoided like the plague.

He'd never allowed himself to feel this depth of emotion for a woman before. He'd always dated women like Alessandra, safe, predictable choices who wouldn't cause waves in his life, because it hadn't been a luxury he could afford. But maybe, he acknowledged, it went deeper than that.

His parents had loved each other to distraction. Too much so, in his opinion, because in the days following the boating accident which had killed his father, his mother had been so heartbroken, she hadn't had the will to fight for her own life, a critical factor that had determined her survival. She had died days later, leaving him and Ilaria with their own heartbreak.

Maybe he had decided that that level of emotion just wasn't worth it. That he would build a world so impenetrable, so shatterproof, that it could never come crashing down on him like it had that hot afternoon in July. Had built impenetrable walls around his heart to protect himself, walls Jensen had decimated with her intense vulnerability and beautiful smile. And now he didn't know what to do with what he'd been handed. Was navigating uncharted territory—territory he couldn't contemplate negotiating with everything he had resting on his shoulders.

Before his wayward thoughts derailed him completely, he rolled up his sleeves and got to work. It was close to nine when a light knock sounded on the door and Jensen walked in, dressed in an olive-green dress. She closed the door behind her and took up a position leaning against his desk, her concerned gaze resting on his fatigued face.

"Cristiano," she said quietly, "you are exhausted. You've hardly slept this week. If you keep going like this, you won't make it through the rest of the week."

"I'm fine," he murmured, attempting to put up some kind of a fight against the pull he felt toward her, which had never been in doubt, but seemed ten times stronger now. "I'm almost done."

"And what will you have for tomorrow?" She didn't attempt to question why he hadn't come to her, or why he was holding back. He almost thought he read the same elemental wariness in her rich ebony gaze, as if she, too, knew the power of what they shared and its ability to decimate them both. Instead, she cocked her head to the side. "You once gave me a speech about knowing my limits, yet it's clear you don't know yours. Every person at that company is depending on you to pull this off, Cristiano. You need to pace yourself."

He threw down the pen. Raked a hand through his hair. Maybe she was right. His head would likely be much clearer in the morning.

He took her in. The dress she was wearing, one of those deceptively innocent, flirtatious short dresses of hers, that made the most of her undeniably perfect backside. How the olive hue, embroidered with little white daisies, enhanced her sun-kissed skin and devastatingly dark eyes.

"How was the luncheon today?" he murmured, feeling the visceral heat rise between them.

"Good," she replied quietly. "Uneventful. It will play well in the media."

"*Bene*. And the shoot in Cannes. Did you get it straightened out with Tatiana?"

"Yes." She hesitated for a moment, disquiet glittering in her eyes, then plunged on. "I have to be there for another day. Until Thursday. But I will fly back right after that. It's not a problem."

"*Cristo*, Jensen." He blew out a breath. "This timing makes me very uncomfortable. Reschedule the shoot. Let someone else do it. It's not worth the risk."

"It's fine," she insisted. "I will have the jet. I can make it work, Cristiano. *Trust me.*"

He did. She had proven herself to him over and over again. And he wanted what was best for her, because he cared about her that much. *"Bene,"* he agreed. "Do it, then."

"Thank you." She dug her teeth into her lip. Looked loath to speak, but did anyway. "I missed you last night," she admitted huskily. "I didn't sleep well at all."

He crumbled then. Melted completely. Pushed back his chair and beckoned to her. She came to him, slid onto his lap, cupped his face in her hands and kissed him in that way that had always seemed holy between them. He should have stopped it, *would* have stopped it, given there was still a handful of staff roaming the villa, but he didn't have the willpower to deny himself her. Not when she ran her palms over the hard muscles of his thighs under the fine material of his trousers and found the hot, hard length of him aching for her. *Craving* her as he always did.

On the kiss went, burned brighter and hotter. Her name left his throat, raspy and broken. She unzipped him and pushed the skirt of her dress aside. It took him a moment to realize she had nothing on underneath, a fact that made his head want to explode with need, until he realized he had no protection and a smothered oath left his lips.

"It's okay," she murmured against his mouth, "I'm protected." Which had never been a promise he'd elected to accept in the past, given the responsibilities that lay on his shoulders, but in that moment, he could not deny himself what his body was screaming for. And when she took him inside her with a languid tilt of her voluptuous hips, and he was buried in tight, hot, wet velvet, he thought he might lose it, right there and right then, from the pure sensation of it all, because she felt like salvation.

Somehow, he kept his composure, hanging on by a thread, counting backward in his head to maintain some type of control, the connection between them unparalleled as she rode him slow and deep, her eyes on his, his fingers clenched tightly around the arms of the chair. And then she punctuated those slow, sensual, maddening circles with sweet kisses that undid him completely. He held out as long as he could, his body desperate to find release, until the flames threatened to suck him under.

Releasing his death grip on the chair, he found the swollen, slick flesh between her thighs, intent on giving her pleasure. His thumb on the tiny, hot nub he'd come to know intimately, he watched her face as he took her apart with a slow, lazy touch, her beautiful brown eyes glazed with passion, a muffled scream leaving her mouth before he allowed himself his own release, sinking his teeth into the satiny curve of her shoulder as he spilled himself deep inside of her, claiming her in a way he'd never done before. Breaking his last rule.

When they were done, spent and wrapped around each other, when the shudders rippling through their bodies had subsided, he picked her up, her legs wrapped around his waist, and carried her to his bedroom. Once there, he fell into a deep, dreamless sleep, Jensen curved against him, his arm around her waist, his surrender complete.

Jensen woke as the first filtered light of day entered the room, arcing across the massive canopied bed and bathing her in a warm, golden glow. Cristiano had left for the office hours before, intent on finishing the work he'd left undone the night before. She closed her eyes and reveled in the rightness of it all. How adored and protected she felt. How, for once in her life, she felt whole, as if the pieces that had always seemed misplaced inside of her had right-sided themselves. As if she was *enough*.

She snuggled deeper into the silk sheets, basking in the glow. She was terrified to admit she needed him. *Wanted* him. That she was feeling as vulnerable as she was. Had been scared to ask him to give her another day in Cannes, lest she somehow ruin it all. Because she couldn't miss that assignment. Needed to get her career back on track. Dispel the rumors that had been circulating ever since Ariana Lordes had walked in her place in Shanghai and stolen the show. The job *she* had earned. It was a burr that dug itself deep beneath her skin. The need to prove she was still on top. That she was still the *best*. That no one could outshine her in front of the camera.

Feeling lazy and sated from her and Cristiano's passionate lovemaking, which they'd indulged in once more before he'd left, slow and sweet and breathtakingly perfect, Jensen finally got out of bed. Electing not to put on her dress before she showered, and needing java desperately, she padded to the wardrobe and found a white shirt of Cristiano's to slip on. Securing her hair in a ponytail, she went downstairs to the sunny, bright kitchen and opened the cupboard to find her favorite mug, which had somehow made its way to a higher shelf. She stood on tiptoe to retrieve it. Then she poured herself a cup of coffee and was adding a dollop of milk when a hushed gasp sounded behind her.

She spun on her heel, her heart slamming in her chest as she recognized the small, slender, exquisitely dressed female standing in the doorway of the kitchen, her big blue eyes wide. Mouth gaping open, she surveyed Jensen, from the top of her tousled head, down over Cristiano's crisp white shirt, which reached to mid-thigh, to her candy-apple-red-painted toes, glimmering against the dark wood floor.

Jensen wasn't sure who recovered first, her or Alessandra. All she knew was that she somehow had the sense to shove the full cup of coffee onto the counter before she spilled it with her shaking hands. Then decided it must be her, when Alessandra's red-tinted mouth continued to open and close, as if she meant to say something, then stopped to reformulate.

"Dio mio," she finally breathed. "It's true. You *are* sleeping with him. And in his shirt…" She shook her head, china-blue eyes glazed. "You are wearing his *shirt. Santo cielo.* What is happening?"

Jensen curled her fingers around the counter, inordinately aware that Cristiano's shirt only came to mid-thigh, exposing the long, golden length of her legs. That her tousled hair must look like she'd come directly from bed, *his* bed, and her mouth, swollen from the sensual kisses they'd shared, looked vulnerable and well used. Not to mention the bite mark on her shoulder she'd acquired in the height of passion, the too-large shirt gaping at the neckline.

She crossed her arms over her chest and sank back against the counter. Attempted as much composure as she could manage when Alessandra was clearly clad head to toe in designer fabric, her makeup immaculate, her critical gaze assessing. "Alessandra," she murmured, "how lovely to meet you. We haven't had a chance to meet properly in person yet."

The petite blonde's glossed mouth curled. "Perhaps you are too busy making headlines to engage in normal social behavior like the rest of us." She shook her head, her honey-blond curls bouncing, her mouth a hard line. "I have no idea what he sees in you. He must have gone temporarily blind."

Jensen's back stiffened. So it was going to be like that. She'd tried for civil, but clearly civil was not the mood of the day. In the same moment, she wondered if it was the Milanese woman's usual behavior to march into Cristiano's home uninvited. Whether she carried with her such a deeply engrained sense of ownership over Cristiano's life and home, she felt it was within her purvey to do so. Which would have been unnerving, given what she and Cristiano had shared last night, if he hadn't made it clear to her that he and Alessandra were over.

So what was this? A social call?

She set a steady, unwavering gaze on the

other woman. "Cristiano is not home. He went into the office."

Alessandra's chin dipped, a visible hint of disappointment glittering in her eyes. 'I was hoping to find him in. I wanted to speak with him."

"Perhaps you can try the office." *Anywhere but here.* She might be assuming a confident demeanour, but nothing about her felt assured when it came to this woman. She reeked of aristocratic authority. It was written across her cultured face. While Jensen felt every inch the scandalous reality show trash Alessandra so clearly believed her to be. "Unless," she offered, "there is something I or Filomena can help you with."

That felt like a stretch, but she tried to keep it cordial. Unfortunately, her words lit a fire under the woman opposite her, her blue eyes flashing against her delicate, finely boned face. "I wouldn't get too comfortable if I were you," she bit out. "Do you really think he's going to take a relationship with you seriously? Cristiano might be having a little fun with you. *Sowing his wild oats* as his grandmother believes he is doing. Perhaps you have seduced him into this—" she waved a hand at her, her face contemptuous "—*fling* with you. But that is all it will ever be. Cristiano will make the right match for himself and for the company, and trust me, that choice will not be you."

Oh my God. The color drained from Jensen's face, until she was sure she was chalk white, the blow the other woman had lobbed at her landing squarely in her solar plexus, stealing her breath. She could not believe she'd just said that. But perhaps what hurt more was Marcella's assessment of the situation. That Cristiano was *sowing his wild oats,* exactly as she'd feared. That no one except him seemed to think this relationship was going to last, and she wondered if that, in itself, was wishful thinking.

It stirred up every fear, every insecurity she'd ever had, anxiety sliding through her blood like a red tide, heating her skin. Because she knew he'd been holding back this last couple of days, fighting his feelings. She'd seen it in his eyes. Watched him battle it. Why it had taken all her courage to seek him out like she had. To put herself out there like that.

Forcing herself to remain calm, she hauled in a deep breath, pulling oxygen into her lungs. "I don't think you have any idea what Cristiano and I share," she finally said quietly. "But thank you for the warning. I will take it into consideration. Now, if you'll excuse me, I have packing to do."

Jensen flew to Cannes the next day, still reeling from her confrontation with Alessandra, which had severely eaten away at the confidence she'd had in her and Cristiano. She was afraid that Alessandra was right. That Cristiano might desire her, might want her, that had never been in doubt, maybe he'd even convinced himself that she was what he wanted. But how could that ever be enough for him? He loved his family. *Adored* them. And Marcella disliked her, despite her latent praise. Cristiano would always do the right thing, just as Alessandra had said he would. How could she ever think he would do otherwise?

How long would it take for Cristiano to realize his mistake? For him to discover she wasn't at all a suitable woman to have at his side? She wasn't stupid enough to think the headlines would stop overnight. That she could control them, when the tabloids would just make something up in the absence of any real news. It had been an omnipresent force in her life.

She and Cristiano had amazing chemistry. But what happened when that passion faded and they entered the reality stage of their relationship? She'd seen what had happened to her parents' marriage when that kind of passion faded. Her mother and father had been completely incompatible. What had happened to Ava's marriage when the glitz and glamour had dissipated and the reality of who she'd married had set in.

Everything had fallen apart. Everything always fell apart.

She'd insisted Filomena not tell Cristiano about Alessandra's visit, because it was the last thing he needed on his mind with everything else he had on his plate. A similar promise she made to herself, as she slid into the car her client had sent to the Nice airport, and traveled to the luxury hotel on the beach in Cannes, where she'd been reserved a lovely suite with a gorgeous view of the Mediterranean Sea. She was going to focus on work and work only, and not let her insecurities rule.

The shoot began at the crack of dawn the following morning on one of the Riviera's most beautiful beaches. Hidden away from the masses of tourists and accessible only via a steep set of steps that numbered in the hundreds, it was a trek to get to the spot the photographer had chosen, a spectacular locale set between two scenic cliffs. She was exhausted by the end of the first day, with the unrelenting heat beating down on her, the weather unseasonably hot for early September.

She collapsed into bed at nine in her air-conditioned suite, only to wake to a second day with more of the same. The end in sight, she marshaled her reserves and fought through the day, which didn't end until well after sunset. Beyond relieved the shoot was over, she returned to her hotel and packed her things, intent on getting to the airport early. She had just slipped the last couple of things into her bag when her cell phone rang. Glancing at it, she absorbed the name of her mother's agent flashing across the screen.

Wondering why Natalia would be calling her, she almost ignored it, given the car waiting downstairs. But something told her to pick up the call. The panic in Natalia's voice chilled her blood. "I heard you are in Cannes shooting. I need your help. Your mother is on a bender and I'm afraid of what she might do. The producer just called and said it's a mess. Your father announced he is marrying some young Hollywood starlet half his age, and she has completely lost it."

Jensen absorbed the somewhat familiar scenario, which had played out far too frequently in her life, her father and the cavalcade of young actresses he'd gone through. That he was remarrying was new and rather startling. She was sure her mother was devastated, because it hadn't been her decision to end things. She still loved him. But that couldn't be her problem right now. Right now, she had to get back to Milan.

She rubbed a palm against her temple. "She is *here?* In Cannes?"

"Yes. They announced next year's jury. Your mother is on it. There was a party afterward. I don't know if she's off her meds or what, Jensen. But it's messy."

Her mind raced, searching for solutions. "Natalia," she murmured, "I can't get caught up in this. I'm about to catch a flight back to Milan. FV is closing Fashion Week tomorrow night and I am headlining the show. You're going to need to handle this one."

"I wish I could, but I'm in New York in meetings and no one there is capable of getting through to her. The usual producer is off, and Veronica doesn't know the new one." The agent paused, swallowed hard. "She is out of it, Jensen. I mean *out of it*. I don't know what's wrong with her. What she's going to do. I've never seen her like this. I'm afraid she's going to destroy her reputation."

Her stomach sank. This could *not* be happening. Tonight, of all nights. But now, she was scared, too, her heart racing in her chest. "Why don't you get Nancy, the assistant producer, to talk to her? She likes her. She may listen to reason if she knows it will affect the show."

"They stopped filming an hour ago. Someone decided it might be inflaming the situation."

Jensen's blood ran cold. They never stopped filming. *Ever*. Drama was great TV.

She frowned. "What do you mean, destroying her reputation? What is she doing?"

"Apparently, she's had a lot to drink on top of the lack or excess of medication. She told Umberto Riccetti he is a misogynistic pig who never knew how to pick his actresses. Riccetti then told everyone she never had any talent and blacklisted her from his events. It's like she's blazing a trail of destruction through the entire party."

Oh God. Jensen wiped a palm over her brow. She could not let her mother disintegrate in front of half of the French Riviera. She would never recover from it. Nor would it aid her efforts to get her mother back on her own two feet.

She didn't have a choice. She had to get her mother out of there. She glanced at her watch. She was early for her flight. With luck, she could make it to the party, retrieve her mother and still get to the airport on time. The key thing was to remove her from the situation before she did any more damage.

"Okay," she murmured. "I'm on my way. Where's the party?"

Cristiano exited his last media interview, the business reporter having peppered him with hard-edged questions that had flayed an inch off his skin by the time she'd concluded. Which had not been unfounded. Francesco Vitale had lost ground to its competitors in the lead-up to Pascal's launch, and his deal with Nicholas Zhang, which would have shored up skepticism about the company's ability to compete on a global scale, was still mired in red tape. Everything, it seemed, was dependent on how Pascal Ferrari's debut collection for FV was received tonight.

Key to which was Jensen, who would wear the most dazzling creations of the evening. Out with Nicholas Zhang and his family for dinner the previous night, he'd missed her call to tell him she had altered her plans because of an issue with the shoot, and would travel back to Milan with Giselle, her client, the following morning. Which had been infuriating enough, given her promises. Then had come the photos of her partying it up on the Riviera with her friends, blowing up his stack of daily clips this morning, which had sent his blood pressure soaring.

He never should have given in to her demands to do that shoot. Should have listened to his instincts, given everything that could go wrong. Given this was the night that could make or break his company. *Santo cielo.*

Lengthening his stride, he strode from the media center to the tent that housed the models and designers as they prepared for the show in the historic Piazza del Duomo, a legendary Fashion Week setting. Featuring the stunning, sparkling Gothic Duomo di Milano cathedral as a backdrop on a perfect Milanese night, the tent was buzzing with activity. Sofia, his assistant, materialized the moment he walked in, the look on her face sending a wave of foreboding through him.

"Where is she?" he bit out.

"She was grounded in Nice until twenty minutes ago, because of the weather. She left you a voice mail."

A dark curl of fury unfurled inside him, twisting itself around his insides, along with a soul-deep, bitter disappointment, because he'd believed in her. He'd truly thought she wouldn't let him down. That she would prioritize him over everything else, particularly given the bond they had created—one he'd thought was special and real. Instead, she had gone out partying the night before, to hell with the responsibilities that lay ahead, had *lied* to him about what she was doing, and now she was going to miss the show.

He listened to the voice mail, heat blanketing his skin. Jensen's voice was husky and halting,

"Cristiano… I'm so sorry. We've been grounded all afternoon. I don't think I'm going to make it. I will call you as soon as I land." Another drawn-out silence, then she whispered, "I don't know what to say."

He didn't either, to be honest. The fury pulsing through him threatened to make his head explode. His twenty-million-dollar bet, the bet he'd fought Francesco tooth and nail for, the bet he'd staked his reputation on, the face of his brand, was MIA. For the biggest show in FV's history. He wanted to lose his shit. But now was not the time, with forty-five minutes left to the show. They had to replace her.

Pascal and his assistant were up to their ears in models and last-minute fittings in the frenetic dressing area, when Cristiano pulled the designer aside with a curt nod of his head. "Jensen's flight just got out," he relayed tersely. "The storms lasted all afternoon. You need to replace her."

Pascal whitened beneath his deep olive skin. "You are sure? There is no chance she'll make it?"

"It's doubtful. You have a contingency plan?"

The designer nodded, his dark eyes troubled. "*Si*. I was holding on for her with the last couple of dresses. I'll make those alterations now. Serafina Bianchi can take her place."

Cristiano nodded. "Do it."

Jensen arrived at the Piazza del Duomo as the FV after-party shifted into full swing. Sick to her stomach about everything that had happened, concerned about her mother, who was still out of it and with a doctor, not to mention the couple of hours' sleep she'd had, curled in a chair by her mother's bed while she watched over her, she felt like a zombie. She wound her way past security and checked in with Pascal. He looked so bitterly disappointed in her, she followed his instructions to don a backless bronze sequined gown he'd designed for the party, without uttering another word.

She peered in the mirror as Stella, her makeup artist, did a superhumanly quick application of color. Registered her unhealthy pallor. She looked downright haggard. It wasn't something Stella could fix, however magical her work, though she did her best as she filled Jensen in on the rumor mill working itself into a frenzy about her absence tonight.

Photos were circulating from the Riviera party the night before, as she'd attempted to blend in and extract her mother while drawing the least attention of the crowd. A photo of her sitting on a not-so-gentlemanly man's knee, his status as a friend of her client's necessitating a polite if firm response from a sharp-toed stiletto, particularly damning. And another from this morning as she'd left the hotel, shattered, a baseball cap pulled down over her eyes.

Oh my God. A buzzing sound filled Jensen's ears. What must Cristiano think? Pascal? She hadn't been able to physically talk to Cristiano to explain anything, and she could only imagine how it looked. Even Stella was eyeing her speculatively, a curiosity she couldn't satisfy. Her mother needed help, but it needed to be private, discreet assistance, not headlines that would ruin her career.

On what might be the only positive note, Stella informed her the response to Pascal's collection had been fantastic, thunderous applause following the designer down the runway, an American fashion guru who ran one of the industry's most prestigious magazines, calling the collection "pure modern genius." Which seemed to be the prevailing opinion.

After Stella pronounced her "as good as it gets," she left the tent and joined the buzzing crowd of glitterati, winding her way through the throngs of people to the VIP group Cristiano stood at the center of, which consisted of Nicholas Zhang, his wife, Claudia, and Ming Li, as well as Marcella, Ilaria and the director of Milan Fashion Week.

Cristiano, his sapphire eyes piercing, stood back as she arrived and held out his arm. Not one physical signal gave away his current frame of mind, except the fury glittering in his eyes.

And she knew, as he pressed a kiss to both of her cheeks, that he was going to pretend that everything was fine in an effort to salvage something from the evening, and she couldn't say she minded because she'd never seen him so furious.

She did her job, despite the ice-cold reception from Marcella and Ilaria's clear confusion over her actions, and spent the night attempting to dazzle the Zhang women and make up for her botched promise. The evening seemed to drag on for an eternity as the attendees toasted Pascal's success, one she had always known was predetermined. Her nerves built with every moment Cristiano stayed silent in that supremely controlled, utterly furious way of his that sank into her bones and raised goose bumps on her skin.

Finally, as the party ended, well into the early hours of the morning, the sun starting to rise in the sky, she could stand the nerves no longer. "Cristiano—"

"Not one word," he bit out, his fingers sinking into her forearm. "We will discuss this when we get home."

Back in the quiet, deadly silent confines of the villa, Jensen deposited her bronze clutch on the front entryway table and followed Cristiano into the salon. Pouring himself a glass of water, he turned and leaned against the bar, fury lighting his eyes. "I only asked one thing of you," he rasped. "That you deliver on your promises to me, Jensen. That you *come through* on this for me. But you couldn't even do that. Instead, it was more important for you to party on the Riviera and drink yourself into a stupor."

Her heart sank, ending up somewhere above her churning insides. "I didn't drink myself into a stupor. I wasn't drinking at all. I was at that party because the shoot had run late and Giselle, who'd offered to get me home in the morning, was attending. I never would have stayed if I'd known this would happen."

Cristiano stared at Jensen, sure she was lying. A shoot only ran so late before the light faded. She should have been on that jet, not at that party. As for not drinking, he'd seen the champagne glass in her hand in those paparazzi photos. Her sitting on another man's lap, which might be enraging him the most, because he cared about her on a level that was unprecedented for him, one he refused to admit even to himself. And then, if that hadn't been enough, there had been the photos from this morning, in which she'd looked gray and hungover.

She looked uncertain and guilty. He knew her intimately enough now to read those emotions. Although to be honest, he wasn't sure he knew her at all. Not if she'd do this to him. "That's why you *plan* for things to happen," he bit out. "That's why I made those rules you thought were so silly. Because this was the one thing that *could not* happen." He raked his fingers through his hair, struggling to focus through bleary eyes. "You humiliated me in front of the media, in front of my investors, in front of the *Zhangs*. You've stirred up a hornets' nest of gossip the company does not need, when Pascal's success needs to rule the day. And for what? So you can party on the Riviera? *Dio mio*, Jensen. Has what we've shared not meant anything to you?"

She stared at him with those wide, beautiful ebony eyes. "Cristiano—you have to let me explain."

"Explain what?" He spread his hands wide. "Give me one reason, *one reason* why you would have done this to me. And maybe I can understand."

She sank her teeth into her bottom lip. Looked to be searching for an answer, perhaps one that would satisfy him. Which sent the fury blanketing him surging through his veins. "Funnily enough," he growled, "the network has been tweeting pictures of you all day. I assume this is going to make it into a storyline for the show?"

"It might, yes, but—"

That made something inside him snap, his low growl cutting her off. He could not handle one more lie. Not one more thing in this moment that disillusioned him even more about her, because he was in *love* with her. Had been for a while. Had taken a chance for once in his life, at having something more, only to have it blow up in his face. Because really, he should have known better.

He couldn't believe he'd allowed it to happen. That he'd allowed himself to be seduced by her beautiful smile and body, by that delicate vulnerability about her that had made him lose his head when he'd needed it the most. Because clearly, he had not been thinking rationally. He hadn't been thinking at all.

Maybe she couldn't help herself. Maybe he'd always known it was her Achilles' heel. But he'd hoped it could be the alternative. That he'd known where her heart was. Which clearly, he hadn't.

He held up a hand. "I don't want to hear it. I am exhausted and I am *done*."

Her eyes widened. "Done? What do you mean?"

He inserted a hard edge to his voice, because it was the only way he could get the words out of his mouth with conviction. "Done with us, Jensen. I thought that maybe you could be what I needed, but clearly, I was mistaken. You aren't even remotely capable of filling that role. Clearly, I was delusional to think so."

Her delicate face crumpled. She stepped toward him, her fingers resting on his arm. "Cristiano—"

He took a step back, away from all that gilded temptation. "Get some sleep. Do your job, Jensen. That's the only thing I want from you."

CHAPTER EIGHT

JENSEN ARRIVED BACK in New York on a steamy, late-summer evening, in a brief few days' respite from her schedule, after which she was due to close Fashion Week in Paris for FV at the end of the week. It had been too difficult to remain in Milan, on the estate, after everything that had happened, with even Filomena giving her the cold shoulder, as if she'd let her down, too, in the worst way possible.

She was heartsick. *Heartsore,* about the spectacular collapse of her relationship with Cristiano. She knew she should have prioritized him and the show over her mother, but she wasn't sure what else she could have done. Allowed her mother to self-destruct in front of half of the French Riviera, decimating what remained of her career, or step in and try and salvage the situation. Either decision had been impossible.

The car drew to a halt in front of her Upper East Side apartment. The sight of the elegant cream-stuccoed town house might have given her some degree of comfort after months on the road had there not been half a dozen paparazzi clustered outside of it, lying in wait.

Salvador, her driver and bodyguard, turned to look at her from his position in the driver's seat. "Do you want me to circle back around? See if we can shake them?"

Jensen shook her head. It was fruitless to even try. And even though the thought of negotiating that gauntlet in her present state of mind was daunting, she had no choice. The photographers had already spotted her, and her sisters were waiting for her inside.

She jammed a baseball hat on her head and pulled it down over her eyes. Braced herself for the impending fracas. Salvador slid out of the car, opened her door and positioned himself between her and the photographers as they walked quickly up the walkway, his hulky, menacing bulk shielding her from the flashbulbs that exploded in her face.

Forced to keep their distance, the paparazzi fired their questions at her, exploding like stray bullets on the night air.

"Why didn't you walk in the show, Jensen?"

"Are you checking yourself into rehab?"

"What's the status of you and Cristiano Vitale? Are you still together?"

The last one physically hurt. Murmuring her thanks to Salvador, she pushed through the front door of her apartment, closing it on a hail of flashbulbs. Ava, her eldest sister, dark-haired and elegant, and Scarlett, her youngest, blonde and rebellious, were waiting in the foyer.

"Can't they leave you alone for one minute?" Ava asked, frowning. "They are like a pack of hyenas."

"There is nothing as scintillating as when a Davis screws up," Scarlett inserted, cynicism staining her voice. "They can't help themselves. It's a national pastime."

Which she'd done more than once over the past few weeks. Jensen threw her purse on the foyer table, too exhausted to move. Ava hooked an arm through hers and drew her into the salon. "You need a glass of wine, and it will all feel better."

She was afraid it was never going to feel better. That Cristiano had torn her from end to end and nothing was ever going to fix it.

She sank down on the white brocade sofa in her favorite room with its beautiful antique fireplace and elegant wood paneling. Ava poured her a glass of wine and pressed it into her hand before leaning back against the fireplace. "Are you okay?"

Scarlett gave Ava a withering look. "Does she look okay? She's been drying mother out again, while her career goes up in flames." She flicked her gaze to Jensen. "What happened with Cristiano?"

"He is furious. I let him down. I let them all down. He told me we are done. That I am not what he wants or needs."

Scarlett sank down on the sofa beside her, her face resolute. "You're done covering for her, Jensen. Destroying yourself for the sake of her, when she doesn't even appreciate it. She just keeps doing it, again and again, because she knows you'll clean up the mess. And Ava and I have let you carry far too much of the load."

"What choice do we have?" Jensen asked wearily. "We can't abandon her."

"Force her to stand on her own two feet. Act like the grown-up she is." Scarlett waved her phone at her. "We have researched a very discreet rehab center in Arizona. They have some of the top specialists in the country. Mom either decides to complete the program during the hiatus, or she doesn't. But the money stops there. You are not putting one more penny of your savings into her, Jensen."

Jensen swallowed hard, because leaving her mother hanging out to dry was a difficult concept to get her head around.

"It's time for you to focus on yourself," said Scarlett. "On your career and, more importantly, on your love life. Surely, things are repairable with Cristiano?"

Jensen's heart pulsed, her misery bubbling over. She told her sisters the whole story then, everything she'd been holding tight to herself these past few weeks, afraid to break what she and Cristiano had. Worried it would somehow vaporize. The home she'd found on the estate with him and Filomena. The stability and grounding she'd discovered with him. The best version of herself she'd allowed herself to be.

"I miss him," she murmured. "I love him. He's everything I never knew I wanted or needed. But I'm afraid I've messed it up too badly to fix it. I lied to him. I didn't prioritize him, and I put the company's reputation in jeopardy. And," she added, her insides still singed, "he made it clear I am not what he wants or needs."

"Because he isn't operating with all the information," Scarlett reproached. "Why didn't you tell him the truth?"

They'd never told *anyone* the truth. It had been far too risky. "We've signed an NDA. The show could sue us."

"Screw the show," Scarlett said baldly. "I'm done letting it ruin our lives."

Jensen sank her teeth into her lip. What if she told Cristiano the truth and he decided it was just another reason he should have nothing to do with her? Because he might, and she wasn't sure she could take another rejection from him, because the last one had been devastating enough. But she wondered if the truth also went deeper than that. To how intensely vulnerable she'd been with him. How much she'd come to need and depend on him. His demands that she trust him and open up to him. How much that had scared her.

Yes, her mother had been in a precarious situation, but it had been *her* choice to protect her, rather than fulfil her obligations to Cristiano. She could say that she'd been putting the bonds of family first, which she had, but she wondered if it had been more than that. That she'd felt so scared about her growing feelings for Cristiano, so afraid to put herself out there, so afraid of being rejected again, she had subconsciously decided to sabotage her relationship with him rather than have him end it first. That she'd told herself she was protecting her mother, when in fact, she had been protecting herself.

The visit from Alessandra had shaken her. Unearthed every insecurity she'd ever had about herself and her relationship with Cristiano. That even if he wanted her, needed her, he would never end up with someone like her, a message he'd driven home in that final conversation they'd shared, in which he'd assumed so much and hadn't given her a chance to explain.

Even if she told him the truth, as Scarlett was urging her to, and he did forgive her, it still didn't change the facts at hand. That Cristiano needed something other than her, and she couldn't live her life waiting for the other shoe to drop.

Cristiano stood looking out at a breathtaking view of the lake from the terrace of the villa on a picture-perfect Milanese night. Nicholas Zhang's signature was on the contract his lawyers had drawn up, his manufacturing issues had been ironed out, and Pascal's collection was garnering rave reviews from every corner of the globe, ensuring the rebirth of the company he had spent a decade rebuilding. Everything he'd worked so hard for, there in the blink of an eye.

He should feel some deeply ingrained sense of vindication. A weight lifted off his shoulders. The chance to perhaps sleep again at night. Instead, his dreams were haunted by a mahogany-haired siren. And she was everywhere. Sitting on the counter in his kitchen, laughing at him with those beautiful dark eyes. Perched on his desk, offering some uncannily sharp observation from that whip-smart brain of hers. In his bed, her long golden limbs splayed out for his delectation, his every fantasy come true.

He knew he looked haunted. He had caught himself staring off into space more than once this week. But he was so disappointed in Jensen, so bitterly disappointed, he wasn't sure he could get past it. He'd been clear he needed honesty from her. Reliability. *Transparency*. It was the only way he could live his life, given his backstory. And yet she hadn't given it to him—she'd given him the opposite.

His fingers tightened around the railing as he took in the sunset setting the sky on fire. He'd broken every rule for her—shattered those carefully delineated lines he drew between business and pleasure. Had gone off script for the first time in his life. She'd been the absolute riskiest choice for him, but he'd done it anyway, because the way he'd felt when he'd been with her had been like nothing else he'd ever experienced. A hedonistic side of himself he'd never tapped into.

He'd known he should listen to his rational self—that she was too much trouble, too young, too *flighty* for him. Had told himself more than once over the past few weeks that he should walk away. Instead, he'd gotten so wrapped up in her, been so mad about her, he hadn't wanted to let her go. Had wanted to keep that piece of himself he'd discovered. To hell with the consequences.

And now she was gone. Restless, unsure of how to handle the unfamiliar emotion bubbling up inside him, how to *shake* it, he carried the glass of scotch to his mouth and swallowed a long draw. The clatter of Filomena's heels on the terrace pulled him out of his reverie. Turning, he absorbed the grimace written across her lined, aged face.

"The *biondina* is here," she said, sottovoce. "I have tried to get her to use the front door, but it doesn't seem to be in her vocabulary."

Cristiano would have smiled at her description of his ex as the *blonde bombshell*, Filomena's feelings for Alessandra long apparent, but he didn't have the heart for it tonight. He wasn't sure he had the patience for it either, but given that Alessandra had already penetrated his inner defenses and was walking out onto the terrace, clad in a chic white pantsuit, he clearly had no choice.

"Va bene," he murmured to Filomena. "Finish up. Enjoy your night."

His housekeeper nodded and vanished inside. Alessandra, an ocean's worth of confidence in her stride, walked across the terrace to greet him. Given their close personal relationship since childhood, a friendship that had eventually turned into a relationship that had been more mutually beneficial than anything, he pressed a kiss to both of her cheeks and summoned a patience he did not possess.

"To what do I owe the pleasure?" he drawled,

sinking back against the railing, arms crossed over his chest, drink pressed to his side. "I thought we were going to see each other at the benefit next week."

Her scarlet mouth firmed. "I thought we should talk, given the events of the past couple of weeks."

His instincts told him to cut it off right there, because this was a path they definitely didn't need to go down, but Alessandra looked as if she had something to say and wasn't about to be derailed.

"Bene," he murmured. "About what in particular?"

"Us." She fixed her china-blue gaze on his. "It is clear that you needed a break, Cristiano. That you've been on a—" she paused, flicking her wrist at him "—how do I say it? A walk on the *wild side*. But it's time we worked things out. You and I both know we are perfectly suited for each other."

Cristiano's mind was boggled. What part of *we are done* had she not understood? How much clearer did he need to be? "We are not getting back together, Alessandra. *Ever.* I thought I made that clear."

She shrugged a shoulder. "You've been under a great deal of pressure. You will change your mind, I'm sure, once you get over this brief lapse of sanity."

Brief lapse of sanity? He eyed her. "You're referring to Jensen, I take it?"

"Si." She crossed a slim leg over the other and rested back against the railing. "I met her. Last week, before Pascal's show. I came to see you, but you weren't here. She came into the kitchen as I was leaving, dressed in one of your shirts, acting as if she owned the place. Honestly, Cristiano, I don't know what you see in her. She is pretty, I will admit, if you are focused on sex appeal. Which is exactly where Marcella thinks the attraction lies. She thinks you are 'sowing your wild oats' with her."

Blood pulsed through Cristiano's head. He couldn't believe his grandmother had said that. But he was more concerned with what Alessandra had said to Jensen. "You talked to Jensen?"

A tiny shrug. "A brief conversation."

"What did you say to her?" he gritted out.

"The truth. That you will never end up with someone like her. That she is just a temporary thing for you while you work your way through whatever it is you are working through. And good that I did, because she has now clearly revealed her true colors." Her voice softened. "I wanted to let you know that I forgive you. I understand that I have been selfish and demanding, and that has been an issue for you. I will work on it. But I think we should choose a wedding date and truly commit, Cristiano. I'm not getting any younger and I know you want to have lots of *bambini*, so we need to do it soon."

Cristiano's head threatened to explode. He could not believe she'd said that to Jensen. That she was so severely deluded. Maybe he'd strung it on too long, maybe part of this was his fault for giving in to the pressure his family had been applying around the match, because in some ways, it had made sense. But *this*, this was so far over the top, he couldn't even comprehend it.

His brain flashed back to the morning Jensen had left for Cannes. She hadn't looked right. She'd looked *off*. He'd brushed it off as stress about the trip, but now, he wondered if it had been more. How must it have felt to hear Alessandra say those things? Given what she'd shared about never being taken seriously by men? How sensitive she was about her family's reputation? Exacerbated by the harsh words he'd uttered when he'd ended things between them, without even giving her a chance to explain. Words he hadn't meant. Words he'd wished he could take back the minute they'd left his mouth.

She must have been devastated. His heart sank deep into his chest. And what had he done to reassure Jensen about his feelings for her?

About his intentions? He'd been so focused on work, on getting through the crunch he'd been in, he'd refused to address his emotions for her. Had been terrified to, because of what that admission might mean. That he was in love with her. Had thought his actions spoke louder than words.

"You can't marry her," Alessandra said dismissively, clearly reading his face. "Honestly, Cristiano. With that video floating around with her mother melting down in France? That family is a disaster waiting to happen."

Cristiano blinked. "What video?"

"Non lo so." I don't know. She waved a hand at him. "Some tacky video someone shot with a cell phone. Veronica Davis was apparently out of it at a party. Drugs, alcohol…who knows? Apparently, she also has massive gambling debt. Jensen had to step in and clean up the whole mess. Can you imagine taking that on?"

No, he couldn't. An unsettled feeling moved through him. Jensen had looked worried, *decimated*, on her return from Cannes. He'd marked it as the guilt she'd felt from letting him down. But now, the pieces of the puzzle he'd been attempting to decipher ever since that first night in London, about Jensen's erratic, contradictory behavior, slotted themselves into discomfiting place. The thirty-thousand-euro bar tab and wrecked hotel rooms in Monaco she had said were some *out-of-control friends*. Her frenetic schedule she wouldn't cut back on. The fear in her voice when she'd called him from France, and said something had come up.

The anxiety he'd sensed in her in the in-between moments when she'd thought no one was watching. She had been and was still covering for her mother, who was, apparently, not only an alcoholic, but a drug and gambling addict as well. Which explained Jensen's insane schedule and need for endless money. She couldn't stop working or the whole thing would fall apart.

He raked a hand through his hair. He'd been so sure he *knew* her. Where her heart was. That he could trust her. And yet what had he done? Believed the worst of her without even giving her a chance to explain. And why would she really? All he had done was throw his autocratic rules at her from day one, dictating what she could and could not do, because she'd led him to believe what he had, clearly to protect her mother. Made it clear where his priorities lay in FV. Nor had he given her any indication she would have his support if she did come to him. That he would have protected her. Because he would have.

She'd told him she found it hard to trust. He

had known that. And yet he'd missed all the signs. Every clue he should have caught.

Jensen had never been on a spiral. Her mother had.

Jensen stood backstage at the Palais Garnier in Paris, the historic Fashion Week setting raising goose bumps on her skin with its gorgeous, gilded interior and ceiling painted by Marc Chagall. Never in her life had she felt this nervous before a show. Anxious, yes, in her first few appearances for big designers, but not this kind of debilitating, bone-deep fear. Her life had exploded around her in the last week, every Davis secret she'd ever harbored on display for the world to see. Lurid, embarrassing details about her mother's descent into gambling and addiction and her decision to enter rehab earlier that week.

Everyone, it seemed, had an opinion about her family's manufactured stardom and their very public fall from grace. But amidst it all, despite her position at the center of the storm, she had a job to do. A promise to keep. And this time, there was nothing to shield her from it. For once in her life, she had to put herself out there. Lay herself bare to the world. Show herself in all of her flaws. And hope she was forgiven.

She took her place at the top of the grand double staircase, Millie on her opposite side, where she would descend, lit by candelabra, to the opulent foyer, and walk the gilded runway. Her knees practically knocking together because she wanted this to be so perfect, to somehow make up for everything she'd done, she drew in a deep breath, waited for her cue, then started down the stairs, flanked by the stunning chandeliers and exquisite bronze sculptures.

The train of the dress in her hand, her concentration complete, so she didn't take a disastrous tumble down the stairs, she absorbed the exquisitely dressed crowd, waiting at the bottom of the staircase. The buzz in the room for Pascal's incredible collection, which was taking the fashion world by storm. But it was the man leaning against one of the massive gold pillars who stole her attention. Dark and insanely good-looking in the tailored navy suit he wore, accented by a pale lavender shirt, he stopped her heart in her chest.

He was not supposed to be here.

Had, according to Pascal, elected to tend to other business, rather than attend the show. Her gaze locked with Cristiano's sapphire-blue one, emotion clogging her throat. What was he doing here, just when she'd finally gotten a hold of herself?

Cristiano's unfathomable gaze slid over the sheer, nearly transparent silver dress she wore, lined only where it absolutely needed to be lined, the slit that began high on her thigh exposing the sweep of her long legs. Over the artfully wild tumble of her dark hair, cascading over her shoulders and down her back. She swallowed hard at the energy that passed between them, the muscles in her throat contracting.

It was undeniable the heat between them. It froze her in her tracks. Sucked the air from her lungs, because that part of them had never been in question. It was everything else that threatened their connection. That her past would always be a barrier for them, no matter how hard, how resolutely, she tried to leave it behind. That being a Davis was a stain on her soul that would forever be a part of her, destroying everything in its wake.

She hiked her chin, holding her head high. She couldn't be anything but who she was. She had finally learned that lesson. But she could define who she was from here on out. And she intended to do just that.

Forcing herself to move, she descended the rest of the stairs. By the time she made it to the bottom, she was shaking in her shoes. It was all she could do to focus for the rest of the show. At the after-party, held in the spectacular Grand Foyer.

She located Cristiano immediately, standing in a group of VIPs, looking immaculately self-possessed as always. Maybe he was here on business, she thought nervously, and it had nothing to do with her at all. Except, why was he looking at her like that, like she was the only person in the room?

Needing something to do, she plucked a glass of sparkling wine from a passing waiter's tray to occupy herself, but Cristiano was already murmuring his regrets to the group he was in and heading toward her, eating up the ground with a purposeful stride.

"Mon Dieu," Millie murmured, her gaze on Cristiano. "I wish a man would look at me like that. Just once."

"He's furious with me," Jensen replied quietly. "I'm not sure you would."

"If that's how he looks at you when he's angry," Millie offered, "sign me up."

Cristiano stopped and greeted them both, the tantalizing citrus scent of his expensive aftershave assailing her senses as he bent his head and pressed his sensuous mouth against her cheek in a whisper-soft caress. It slammed into the protective layers she'd encased herself in, unearthing emotions she didn't want to feel. Memories that held the power to disassemble her completely. She sucked in a breath as he did the same with the other cheek and stepped back, his sapphire gaze fixed on hers, penetrating and unyielding.

"A moment," he murmured, "if you wouldn't mind."

She followed him, knees shaking, as he guided her through the crowd, out to one of the stately balconies, with its superb view of the Place de l'Opéra, deserted as the guests enjoyed a first cocktail inside.

She leaned against a pillar, crossing her arms over her chest as a warm breeze wafted over her, attempting to corral the emotion vibrating her insides. The hurt still bubbling up inside of her like an irrepressible force. Cristiano took up a position opposite her, his gaze trained on her face.

"You aren't supposed to be here," she murmured, bereft as to what to say. Unsure which of the emotions coursing through her it was appropriate to feel. Hope. Fear. Uncertainty. They all seemed relevant.

"I wanted to see you," he said quietly. "And apologize for the way I handled things that night in Milan. I was angry. I said things I shouldn't have. Things I didn't mean. Things I never would have said if I'd known the truth. Which you didn't tell me."

Her lashes lowered, shading her cheeks. "I was protecting my mother."

"Jensen," he murmured on a low note, a banked level of emotion edging his voice that tightened her insides, "we were lovers. As intimate as two people can be. I asked you, *begged* you to tell me the truth. What was going on. I wanted to help. Instead, you allowed me to believe that you had cavalierly broken the terms of your contract, that you didn't care enough to make the show, that you had let all of us down, when in fact, you were cleaning up after your mother, who is an *addict* you have been covering for your entire life. Who is the reason you work yourself into the ground at the expense of your own career." His mouth flattened, a dark brow winging to the sky. "Do I have that right, *cara*?"

"Pretty much." She pushed a hand through the tumbled length of her hair, her stomach clenching. "You were so angry, Cristiano. I didn't think explaining would help. You had made it clear I was not to put a foot out of line or I would lose my contract. I was terrified if I told you the truth about my mother, you would drop me like a hot potato. That you would consider me more trouble than I am worth."

His sapphire gaze darkened. "I *cared* about you, Jensen. If I was autocratic in the beginning, it was because I was protecting my investment. Because I didn't understand what was going on, and you didn't tell me. All that changed when we became lovers. Surely you knew that? Why wouldn't you tell me?"

She drew in a deep breath. "My mother's addictions are a secret we've guarded for years—since early on in the show. She was never quite right after my father left. She was destroyed by it. But she needed the show to survive. The producers were adamant her issues not become public knowledge, because they felt it would ruin the show. Which would have been devastating for her." She sank her teeth into her lip. "My mother is in debt. A great deal of debt. I have been bankrolling her expenses for the past couple of years, attempting to get her back on her feet, yet it never seems to happen."

"Which is why you were so desperate to work. Why you wouldn't take a step back."

"Yes." She inclined her head.

"And the party in Cannes in which you purportedly spent thirty thousand euros on gambling and drinks and trashed hotel rooms... That was not you, but your mother?"

She nodded. "It was easier to let the press think it was me. To draw the attention away from her. Before," she elaborated, "she was more discreet. In control. But these past few months, it all began to spiral. The show was on the ratings bubble. The producers were threatening to cancel if she didn't deliver the numbers for the season finale. It was the only reason I did the fountain stunt. Because she begged me to do it. Her fears about money, the pressure the producers were putting her under. It was crushing. That night in Cannes was a breaking point for her. My father had announced he was remarrying—some Hollywood starlet half his age. She was shattered."

He frowned. "And your sisters? Could they not have helped? Where are they in all of this?"

"They help when they can, but they are managing a fledgling business. There was no money to spare in the early years, nor much time, for that matter. So a lot has fallen on me. Which will hopefully change now that they are more established. We worked out a plan in New York on how to handle things once my mother is out of rehab."

"You should have come to me," he said quietly. "I could have been there for you. I *would* have been there for you. But I can't solve a problem I don't know exists."

She sank her teeth deeper in her lip. "You were in the middle of a tsunami, Cristiano. *Drowning.* I wasn't going to add something else to your plate."

He pushed away from the wall and closed the distance between them, his familiar, delicious scent infiltrating her senses, weakening her knees. "I am in *love* with you, *cara*," he murmured, lifting a hand and brushing his thumb across her cheek. "That's what people do when they care about someone. They put them first. Which is why it hurt so much when you didn't show up for me that night. When you let me down so badly. I couldn't understand why you would do something like that. And you refused to trust me enough to tell me the truth."

Her brain froze at the part where he'd said he loved her. *Loved her.* It was a little too earth-shattering to process. Her gaze locked with his, her heart crawling up her throat. "I have trouble with trust. I told you that. It's something I struggle with."

His gaze softened. "Well, you're going to have to get used to it, because I'm not going anywhere, *cara.*"

Her heart started to race like a runaway train. "You told me I'd never be what you needed that night in Milan, Cristiano. You were fighting your feelings for me. I watched you do it night after night."

"Because I was trying to sort out my feelings. *Process* them. Not because I didn't love you." He raked a hand through his thick dark hair, stark emotion written across his hard-boned face. "My parents loved each other deeply. Ilaria and I were shattered when we lost them. Maybe I decided I was never going to put myself through that pain again. So I chose a woman like Alessandra, who seemed a safe, logical choice. But I couldn't pull the trigger on it."

A glint of humor entered his sapphire gaze. "And then I met you and you whirled through my life like a hurricane, and I discovered a depth of emotion I'd never felt before. A *part* of myself I'd never known. And I knew I could never settle for anything less."

Her knees were feeling weaker with every word that came out of his mouth, dangerously close to giving way beneath her. "I'm so sorry," she whispered. "I know how much that night meant to you. It killed me inside. If I could do it over, find a way to make it right, I would. But I can't."

"I don't need you to do it over," he said softly. "That's one of the things I love so much about you, Jensen—that you love so deeply. That you are still hanging in there with your crazy, misguided mother, when she's given you a million reasons to walk away. Because you value family that much. But there is," he qualified, "one thing I need from you, *cara mia,* if we are to make this work. Honesty. *Full disclosure.* Trust. It's a nonnegotiable for me given my past. I have to know I can depend on you, no matter what."

He was talking about the future. Her brain couldn't seem to process it all, because it felt like a promise. "In exchange," he continued, a solemn expression on his face, "I want to be the man you can always count on. Who will always be there for you. Who will protect you, no matter what. I have broad shoulders, *tesoro*. I can take it."

Her heart thudded in her chest, like it might burst. And then, she thought it might have, when he dropped to one knee right there on the balcony in front of her, in his beautiful dark suit, so handsome he stole her breath, and pulled a satin box out of his jacket pocket.

Oh my God. She sagged against the pillar, knees weak, as he flipped open the box to reveal a sparkling sapphire ring surrounded by diamonds in what appeared to be a deep Vitale blue.

"It seemed fitting," he murmured, capturing her hand in his. "Marry me, Jensen. I'm like a ghost in that damn villa, it's so empty without you. I need you back."

It seemed impossible to get the word out, past the lump in her throat, because he was all she'd never known she could have. And she was afraid he would vaporize like everything else good had done in her life. Except he was so very real as he slid the platinum band over her finger and the beautiful sapphire glittered in the moonlight. And she knew in her heart, it was forever.

"Yes," she finally breathed, acquiring enough

air to speak. And then she was in his arms, her fingers buried in his thick dark hair, and he was kissing her.

Neither of them heard Millie and Lucy traipse along a few moments later, stilettos clicking the stone beneath their feet. Until Millie's audible gasp filled the air. "Oh my God. *Oh my God.* Look at that ring. That is so completely unfair."

Jensen stirred out of Cristiano's soul-searing kiss and smiled against his lips. She liked to think of it as meant to be.

"Go find your own," she tossed over her shoulder. "This one is taken."

"Sure, sure," Millie grumbled. "Tell me where I can find one like that and I will."

* * * * *

If you fell in love with
How the Italian Claimed Her
*then get lost in these other thrilling stories
by Jennifer Hayward!*

A Debt Paid in the Marriage Bed
Salazar's One-Night Heir
Christmas at the Tycoon's Command
His Million-Dollar Marriage Proposal
Married for His One-Night Heir

Available now!